BOUND BY MAYHEM

BEACH BOUND BOOKS AND BEANS
BOOK 5

CHRISTY BARRITT

River Heights

CHAPTER
ONE

"YOUR PAST REMAINS WITH YOU—LIKE either an angel or a demon!" A ghost clothed in tattered white rags swooped past, its voice thin and frail as it croaked out the admonition.

Tali Robinson watched as the actor wearing the sheets nearly crashed into the wall on the side of the stage.

She'd let someone else worry about Arnie. The college student was a handful.

For now, she stood to the side with her friends, quickly catching up before the rehearsal officially started.

Mac MacArthur turned toward them. "Abby couldn't have picked three better ladies to be the angels in this play."

He was talking about Tali, Cadence, and Serena.

The three of them stood in a circle on the stage at the Sandpiper Theater. Someone had brought a crockpot of apple cider, and the spicy-sweet smell of it wafted through the air, along with the scent of the evergreens that lined the stage.

Christmas was only a week away.

Tali felt herself beaming as she adjusted the silver garland halo on her head.

"Aren't you sweet? And she couldn't have picked anyone better to play King Herod either." Tali tapped the oversized crown on the top of Mac's head, marveling at just how adorable he looked dressed as royalty.

Abby Mendez had organized a Christmas play here on Lantern Beach. Her ultimate goal was to start a theater group on the island, and her first task had been writing a short script called *You Scared the Dickens Out of Me.*

The play was a mix of a modern-day *Christmas Carol* with scenes from the nativity intertwined. In Abby's retelling of the story, the Ghosts of Christmas Past, Present, and Future appeared in the form of social media posts to twentysomething Eleanor Kluge.

Abby had received a grant for the play, and she'd used the money for props and to update the technology at the theater. She'd added a screen to the back wall of the stage and a projector at the back of the theater. She used that to flash the social media posts for the audience to see.

The cast and crew had gathered at the island's old theater for a dress rehearsal. The rustic building at one time had been a one-room schoolhouse. It had been shuttered for decades, though, until being renovated about five years ago into a theater.

As it turned out, the theater doors had never opened back then.

Right now, it had been given a second chance.

The play opened in two days, and they'd gotten together to rehearse several different times so far. Now, they needed to put it all together.

Excitement thrummed in the air as people practiced their lines and chatted with one another. Arnie appeared to have recovered from his run-in with the wall quite fine, and now he tried to haunt one of the townspeople—a cute college girl named McKayla.

Tali glanced around and spotted all of her favorite islanders here. Ty and Cassidy Chambers were playing Mary and Joseph, and their little girl, Faith, was baby Jesus. Several members of Blackout, a security agency based on the island, would be shepherds, and one lucky former Navy SEAL got to play an animal.

Speaking of which . . . Axel Hendrix stepped out

with a scowl, and Mac didn't bother to hide his snicker.

"I can't believe I have to play a donkey," Axel muttered.

Olivia Rollins, his girlfriend, laughed as she stepped out beside him and wrapped her arms around his waist. "You're the cutest donkey I've ever seen."

"Well, hearing you say that makes it all worth it then." Axel planted a quick kiss on her forehead.

It seemed everyone was ready to start.

Tali glanced at her watch and frowned. "Why isn't Abby here yet? It's not like her to be late."

"That's exactly what I was wondering." Cadence continued folding some pages of discarded, damaged books. She'd been in the process of learning to make flowers out of the pages.

The scent of the paper reminded Tali of her days as a librarian. There was nothing quite like the smell of old books.

"You haven't heard from her?" Tali asked.

Cadence shook her head. "Abby's been working so hard behind the scenes. Maybe she took a nap before coming here and overslept. It's the only thing that makes sense."

"I can clear this up fast. Let me call her and find

out." Tali pulled out her phone and dialed Abby's number.

But the phone rang and rang before going to voicemail.

She frowned as she clutched the phone and lowered it from her ear.

This wasn't like Abby.

Something was wrong. Tali was certain of it.

————

Ten more minutes passed, but nothing had changed.

Most of the cast and crew continued to chat and goof off amongst themselves while they waited.

But Tali couldn't bring herself to relax.

Mac moved closer and lowered his voice. "Have you tried to call her again?"

Tali nodded. "Several times. She's not answering. That's not like her either. She practically sleeps with that phone beside her."

"Let's give her a few more minutes," Mac said. "If she still doesn't show up, maybe we could swing by her place just to make sure everything's okay. It's probably nothing."

Tali wanted to believe him, but she wasn't sure if she could.

A bad feeling brewed in her gut.

A few minutes later, she glanced around at the thirty or so cast and crew members. Some of their chatter had faded. The more time that passed without Abby, the more the excitement in the air diminished.

Everyone else was growing concerned too, weren't they?

Just then, Police Chief Cassidy Chambers wandered over toward them, adjusting her blue head scarf with one hand and holding Faith with her other arm. "Everything okay?"

"Abby's late, and she isn't answering her phone." Tali glanced at her watch again, her concern continuing to grow.

The frown on Cassidy's face showed she was also concerned.

"I may not be able to stay for the entire rehearsal." Cassidy bounced Faith on her hip as the girl tried to pull off Cassidy's headscarf again. "I've already gotten two calls. Something about the holidays seems to make people act even crazier than usual."

"I'll never forget that one time Brian Jenkins got himself tangled up in Christmas lights while he was using the bathroom. The lights that were strung around the room somehow wrapped themselves around the toilet while he was using it." Mac, the island's former police chief and current mayor, flashed a smile. "I got a call from him at 2:30 a.m. Had to help him get untangled. Talk about memories you never forget."

The group shared a laugh.

"There certainly isn't a shortage of excitement here in Lantern Beach." Tali had only been here six months, but she'd quickly learned that fact.

Her smile faded as she glanced at her watch again.

Abby was now thirty minutes late.

Tali couldn't wait any longer. "I'm going to check on her."

"I'll go with you." Mac stepped closer.

"I can go with you too if you'd like." Cassidy switched Faith to her other hip as her phone buzzed, no doubt with another call from work.

"It sounds like you have your hands full," Mac said. "How about if Tali and I go, but if anything comes up, we'll call you?"

"Okay then." Cassidy glanced at her phone again before shoving it back into her pocket. "I'm going to have Officer Leggott take care of this call. In the meantime, I hope Abby's just having car trouble and forgot to charge her phone or something."

"Let's hope." But Mac's lips flickered as if he were fighting a frown.

CHAPTER
TWO

A FEW MINUTES LATER, after shedding their costumes, Tali and Mac climbed into his truck—a vehicle that was quickly becoming familiar to Tali.

She and Mac officially began dating six weeks ago, and those six weeks had been wonderful. In some ways, it felt as if she'd always known him. In other ways, their relationship still felt so fresh and exciting.

Mac might be in his late sixties, but he was still handsome and spry. She felt certain he could show up most twentysomethings with his wit, intellect, and even his policing abilities.

"Here we go again, Goldie." Mac cast her a look.

He'd taken to calling her Goldie lately, mostly because he said she reminded him of the actress

Goldie Hawn. Tali supposed she could see it. They both had the same blonde hair and thin build.

Before he could crank the engine, the back doors opened.

Tali turned and saw Cadence and Serena slip inside.

"You didn't think you were going without us, did you?" Serena snapped her seatbelt in place before anyone could argue.

Tali wasn't quite sure about casting Serena as an angel. The girl had a good heart, but her methods sometimes left a lot to be desired. She was headstrong and liked to leap before she looked.

Tali and Mac exchanged a glance.

Though the girls were young enough to be Tali's daughters—maybe even her granddaughters—they somehow felt like good friends. Maybe it was their love of books and coffee that had forged such a tight bond beyond the generations.

Either way, they didn't have time to waste right now.

After all seatbelts were latched, they took off down the road toward Abby's place.

Abby had only moved to the island this past summer, and she lived in a duplex located on the Pamlico Sound side of the island, an area where small, less expensive homes were generally located. The roads were mostly dirt or gravel, and the houses less glamorous than the oceanside homes.

As they headed down the road, Tali closed her eyes and lifted a prayer that everything was okay.

All the mayhem that had happened on the island was messing with her mind. Danger wasn't supposed to be around every turn . . . right?

———

Mac didn't like the way any of this was playing out.

Playing out?

He nearly groaned at his mental choice of words.

He was simply accustomed to thinking in worst-case scenarios. That was probably what was happening now as well. As the former police chief, he'd seen his fair share of crimes. As current mayor, he liked to keep a pulse on everything happening on the island.

Besides, sometimes jobs became part of the fabric of your being. Investigating was one of them.

That's why he didn't question the bad feeling that lingered in his gut.

As they rode down the highway cutting through the center of the island, Christmas decorations lit up numerous houses, reminding him again of the upcoming holiday. The island residents liked to go all out with community events.

They'd already had the Lantern Beach Grand Illumination, which included participants walking down the boardwalk carrying lanterns alongside carolers dressed in traditional historical garb. The celebration honored the island's history, which included lanterns —hence the name. At the end of their walk, a twenty-foot Christmas tree was lit in the town's common area.

It was one of his favorite traditions.

Just then, they pulled up to Abby's place.

The duplex stood on stilts—as did most of the homes on the island—and had cedar siding that looked gray and curled with age. Two sets of stairways stood guard on either side of the place, one for each front door.

Abby had mentioned just last week while at Tali's place that her duplex neighbor had moved back to Florida for the winter. Her other neighbors on either side had colorful lights strung around their homes as well as several inflatables in their yards. One was a humongous Grinch, and another was Charlie Brown.

Mac wondered if they were having some type of competition.

He turned his gaze back to Abby's place.

Her car still sat out front.

Mac hoped that was a good sign. Maybe she had just taken a nap and overslept.

They all climbed from his truck and hurried up the steps to her front door.

But when they reached it, the door wasn't latched.

They exchanged glances.

That wasn't like Abby.

Mac's muscles tightened as he reached for the doorknob. "Let me go first."

As he slipped inside, the ladies followed close on his heels.

He couldn't blame them for wanting to rush in. They were worried about their friend.

Pausing near the entry, he scanned the place.

He didn't like what he was seeing.

A table had been turned over. A lamp lay broken on the floor. An opened present sat on the coffee table, torn paper all around it. A glass of water had fallen over and spread across the tile floor.

It appeared as if a struggle had happened here.

"Oh, Mac . . ." Tali gasped and grabbed his arm.

Then she sucked in another breath and pointed to something in the distance.

"Is that . . . blood?"

He followed her gaze and saw the spatter of red in the kitchen.

His jaw tightened.

He didn't like the scenarios racing through his mind.

CHAPTER
THREE

"SOMETHING HAS HAPPENED," Tali muttered as she stared at the red splotches on the kitchen table. "Something bad."

Serena and Cadence clutched each other as they stood near the kitchen door.

"Stay here." Mac's voice hardened with authority. "I'm going to check out the rest of her place."

Tali knew what he was getting at.

If he found Abby, he didn't want them to see her. Especially if she was injured or . . .

Tali couldn't bring herself to finish that thought.

"What do you think happened here?" Serena glanced around, her eyes wide, curious, and concerned.

"I don't know." But Tali was thinking in worst-case scenarios.

As she glanced down the hallway waiting for Mac to return, she barely saw Serena gravitating toward the kitchen.

She should stop her. Tali knew she should.

But all she wanted was to talk to Mac. To hear him say everything was okay.

That was all that mattered right now.

As Mac returned to the room, his attention snapped toward Serena. "What are you doing, girl?"

Tali looked over in time to see Serena press her finger into the blood and then lick it.

"Serena!" she muttered in horror.

"It's okay." Her gaze lifted. "It's raspberry jam—although it turned out more like a purée. Abby told me she was thinking about making some thumbprint cookies today. This isn't blood."

Relief whooshed through Tali.

That was good news, at least.

"Abby's not back there?" Tali's voice caught. "She didn't fall asleep or something?"

"No." Mac's jaw hardened. "No, she's not here."

Tali wasn't sure if that was a good thing or a bad thing.

"What about her purse?" Tali asked. "Her phone? Did you see them?"

He shook his head. "I didn't."

Mac paced closer to the coffee table and slipped

on a glove—yes, he always carried them with him. Carefully, he dipped a hand into the already opened gift box.

Then he pulled out . . . a piece of coal.

"It appears someone thinks Abby has been very naughty this year." Mac frowned as he stared at the rock in his hand.

"Who would give her coal?" Serena nibbled on her bottom lip as she contemplated the question.

"Maybe it was a joke." Cadence half shrugged as if hopeful—but doubtful—her theory was correct.

"Look at the note on top of the box." Tali pointed to the piece of paper there.

The past always finds a way back to you. Bah, humbug!

Tali frowned.

She didn't like the sight of this.

————

Cassidy had shown up several minutes ago and now examined Abby's place as the rest of the crew stood outside.

Mac tried to keep their thoughts occupied, but he knew everyone was worried, and he couldn't blame them. He was worried too.

His thoughts shifted as he snapped into police

mode. "Do any of you know if Abby was having problems with anyone?"

They remained quiet for a moment until finally Cadence spoke. "She did tell me that she dated some guy when she lived in Myrtle Beach a while back. But something happened between them. She said she didn't like to talk about it."

Tali frowned. "Abby is secretive about her past. She didn't talk about it much, other than to say she was involved in community theater."

That was interesting. "But she hadn't seen this guy around here, right?"

Cadence shook her head. "Not that I know of. I think she would've mentioned it if she did."

"Did she tell you his name?" Mac asked.

"Yes, she mentioned it." Cadence said. "Michael Something or other."

"I'll see if I can figure out his last name and look into him." Mac paused. "What about the way she's been acting lately? Anything out of the ordinary?"

"She has seemed rather stressed, but I figured it was just because of this Christmas production." Serena shrugged. "I know it's taking up a lot of her time, and she really wants it to go well so she can get off to a good start with the theater group."

"That makes sense," Mac muttered. "But she didn't seem to be frightened of anything, correct?"

A neighbor's Christmas display suddenly began playing music—"Up on the Housetop"—and it seemed way too cheerful.

Mac had his gun with him, and he was halfway tempted to shoot it. He wouldn't. But he *was* tempted.

Again, they all looked at each other before shrugging.

"She hasn't told me anything." Cadence shivered. "In fact, I talked to Abby just a couple of hours before rehearsal was supposed to start, and she sounded fine. She was going to take a quick shower, get changed, and then head to the theater early to get things ready. She sounded excited."

Tali rubbed her arms as if chilled. "I don't like this."

Mac knew they shared that sentiment.

Tali peered up at him with worry in her eyes. When she looked at him like that, he knew he'd do anything to make things right for her again.

"What can we do, Mac?" Tali's voice cracked with underlying tension.

"We can start looking, see if we can find her."

"That sounds like a plan." Tali's expression remained pensive. "I just can't justify standing around here and not doing anything. Not while she could be out there somewhere hurt or in danger."

As she said the words, her phone buzzed. So did Cadence's and Serena's.

They all glanced at their cell phones at the same time.

It was a text from an unknown number.

They put their phones together to compare what they'd all gotten.

The messages matched.

> The real scrooge of Christmas is Abby herself.

They all exchanged glances.

Why would someone send this text to them about Abby? Even more so—who had sent it? Who had all of their numbers?

And where was Abby right now?

Mac didn't think that Abby had gotten cold feet before the play.

She wasn't the type.

No, the extrovert was the kind to bask in the limelight.

More unease churned inside him.

He didn't like the way this was looking.

CHAPTER
FOUR

TALI'S WORRY grew with every passing moment. She and Mac rode around in his truck, searching the island for Abby.

Mac had dropped Serena and Cadence off at the theater so they could get Cadence's car. Those two would also scour the island in an effort to divide and conquer. Cassidy and her officers were searching as well.

At times, their makeshift investigation felt futile. What did Tali expect? To see Abby wandering down the road by herself? Standing outside someone else's house practicing one of her accents in front of some kind of North Pole display?

Abby was known for practicing various accents as a means of getting into character and keeping her acting abilities sharp.

The chances of randomly finding her seemed unlikely.

But Tali had to do something. She couldn't simply go back to her apartment and wait to hear some news. In that sense, driving around was better than doing nothing.

Mac squeezed her hand. "I know you're worried."

Tali loved the strong feel of his fingers as they intertwined with hers. Meeting Mac after she'd come here had been such an unexpected blessing.

She wasn't looking for love. And she *definitely* hadn't been anticipating meeting someone as fantastic as Mac. He brought so much goodness and fun and stability to her life. Sometimes, Tali still pinched herself as she wondered if what the two of them shared was too good to be true.

"I just know that something's not right." Tali rubbed her arms, a chill washing over her. "I want to help."

"We are. We're doing what we can. Hopefully, we'll hear from Abby soon."

"Do you think Cassidy will have any luck tracking her phone?" Tali stared out the window at the cheerful Christmas lights as they passed. She usually loved riding around town and looking at displays. Right now, it seemed frivolous.

Mac made a clucking sound with his tongue before offering a half shrug. "That's hard to say. It can take a while to get approval for those things. Who knows if Abby still even has her phone?"

Tali held back a frown. She didn't like the sound of that. But she knew Mac was telling the truth, and that was what she wanted. She didn't need people kowtowing around reality in order to make her feel better.

"What are we going to do about the play if we can't find her?" Tali knew the question was completely inconsequential right now.

The play didn't really matter. Not when Abby was missing. But just for practical purposes—and to have something to distract herself from her thoughts —she decided to concentrate on that for a moment.

"People have already bought tickets," she continued. "That money is supposed to go to Hope House."

Hope House was the charity run by Ty Chambers, a former Navy SEAL. The organization helped veterans who were struggling to integrate back into civilian life.

"We will cross that bridge when we get there." Mac gripped the steering wheel. "For now, we just keep looking."

As soon as he said the words, someone darted into the road right in front of them, waving his arms.

As Mac threw on the brakes, Tali prayed his truck stopped before colliding with the person.

———————

Mac's heart rate ratcheted as the truck skidded to a stop.

Without hitting the pedestrian on the road.

He let out several deep breaths as he collected himself.

"What was this guy thinking?" he muttered. "He could've been killed."

The man's face came into view, and Mac recognized the person as Tank—the man who owned the surf shop next door to Tali's place, Beach Bound Books and Beans.

The man's eyes were wide, and a sweatband was stretched across his shaved head.

Based on his sweatpants and ear pods, he was jogging. He also wore his customary tank top—his regular attire no matter the weather.

"Stay here," Mac muttered.

He climbed from the truck, slammed the door, and strode up to Tank. "I could've hit you."

Tank—a reformed pothead, avid surfer, and seasoned business owner—ran a hand through his scraggly goatee. "I know. Sorry. I saw you heading down the road." He stepped from side to side as if anxious. "I needed to get your attention before you drove past. Otherwise, I wouldn't have—"

"What's going on with you, Tank?" Mac couldn't stand here and listen to him blabber like this all day. "Why do you seem frantic?"

"I think I saw Abby." He sucked in a few shallow breaths. "I heard you were looking for her."

Now he had Mac's attention. "Where did you see her?"

"By the ferry dock. At least, I think it was her. But she was sitting against a streetlight with her knees to her chest, and she looked upset. I didn't know if I should approach her or not so I—"

"You did the right thing stopping us," Mac said. "Although, next time try waving your hands from the side of the road. Or call someone for help."

Tank nodded. "I would have, but I was out for a jog, and I misplaced my phone, so I couldn't call anyone."

Mac climbed back in his truck, anxious to know if Tank was right.

As soon as Tank was out of the way, Mac put his truck in Drive.

"What's going on?" Tali stared at him with curious eyes.

"Tank thinks he saw Abby. I'm going to go check it out now."

"Really?" Tali's voice pitched higher with hope.

And Mac hoped that this update didn't in any way let her down.

CHAPTER
FIVE

ADRENALINE SURGED THROUGH TALI.

Had Tank really seen Abby?

They couldn't get to the ferry docks fast enough to find out.

Finally, probably three minutes later, Mac pulled up.

As he did, his headlights illuminated a figure leaning against the light pole. Just as Tank had said, the woman's knees were pulled to her chest and her head buried in her arms.

Despair.

That was all Tali could think about.

The person sitting there was the picture of despair.

But what she wasn't sure about was whether or

not that person was Abby. Her hunched, balled-up position made her identity hard to determine.

"I'm going to check this out first." Mac reached for the door handle.

"But—"

Mac's gaze locked with hers. "As soon as I know everything's okay, I'll motion to you. I promise."

Tali frowned but nodded.

She appreciated his protectiveness. But she also appreciated the fact that Mac respected her and didn't try to tell her what to do. She'd been on her own for a long time, so having someone try to boss her around sounded awful.

She watched as Mac approached the woman and leaned toward her. When the person raised her head, the streetlight illuminated Abby's face.

And she looked terrible.

Before Mac could even motion to Tali, she opened the door and scrambled toward her friend.

Abby was trying to say something, but her words were so mangled with sobs they were hard to make out.

Tali knelt in front of her. "You've got to slow down, sweetie."

Abby wiped her swollen, red eyes. As she did, she glanced at Mac.

Tali knew what that look meant.

Abby wanted privacy as they talked.

Mac got the hint and nodded before taking several steps back. But he remained close enough just in case things turned ugly.

Tali turned back to Abby. The twenty-seven-year-old was beautiful, with Italian features—dark hair, olive skin, and a big personality.

Tali had never seen her look so defeated.

"Why don't you start again?" Tali asked quietly.

Abby's face crumpled with grief. "Oh, Tali . . . you're going to hate me."

Tali's heart skipped a beat with alarm. "Hate you? I could never hate you. My sweet girl . . . what is it that has you so downtrodden?"

Tali had a feeling this had to do with something more than just Abby's ransacked house.

When she still didn't say anything, Tali added, "We thought something had happened to you. We've been looking for you. It looked like a fight happened in your house, and there were even red drops on the kitchen counter."

She wiped her eyes using the sleeve of her over-sized sweatshirt. "I was making thumbprint cookies for the play practice tonight. Then I found a present at my door."

"The coal, right?"

She nodded. "I thought it was just a joke or something. But immediately afterward, I got the email with that video link. Seeing it freaked me out. I knew I had to leave the house for a while. On the way out, I knocked the table over—a glass of water was on it—and then the lamp fell. It was pretty much a disaster, each mistake having a domino effect, but I didn't want to take the time to clean it up."

Tali wondered what kind of video Abby was talking about.

She was going to have to wait for Abby to compose herself before she found out.

————

Ten minutes later, Tali managed to convince Abby to go to the bookstore and coffeehouse to get out of the cold and get something warm to drink.

Meanwhile, Mac had made the calls to everyone to let them know Abby had been found and was safe.

As they headed down the road, Tali had no doubt that Serena and Cadence would be waiting at Tali's place when they got there. Rehearsal had apparently been canceled.

Mac had asked Cassidy to come later—after they talked to Abby more.

There may not have been a crime here—especially

if Abby had left her place trashed like she did. If what she said was correct, all of this had been precipitated by some kind of email. Maybe they needed to tap the brakes and stop thinking in catastrophic scenarios.

When they arrived, Mac ushered them inside. Serena and Cadence, just as she'd suspected, had been waiting on the boardwalk for them. The girls filed into the bookshop with them.

They led Abby to the comfiest chair. Then Tali fixed everyone coffee and tea. Once the group was settled, Tali picked up her Westie, Sugar, and placed the dog in her lap.

Then they waited to hear what Abby had to say. Mac lingered in the background, giving them space but still listening.

Abby wiped her eyes, not looking like the vivacious, enigmatic actress they all knew and loved.

She sniffled before saying, "Someone posted a video about me online and sent me the link."

"What kind of video?" Tali's thoughts raced.

"It's just horrible." She wiped her eyes again as another sob escaped.

Tali had no idea what Abby might have done or what kind of video she might have seen that would be this horrible. But she kept her mouth shut and waited.

"Can we see it?" Serena asked. "You know we're not going to judge you."

"You're not going to be able to stop yourselves from judging me." Abby pressed her eyes closed as if she couldn't bear that thought.

What could be so terrible? Tali's imagination instantly went to murder or some type of vicious bullying incident or something.

After a few minutes of convincing, Abby pulled up her phone and found the email she was talking about.

Tali braced herself as Abby clicked the link and hit Play.

CHAPTER
SIX

MAC WAS MOSTLY TRYING to mind his own business. But if something was going on here, he wanted to know about it.

Right now, the video was buffering, and everyone was waiting with bated breath for it to begin.

Including him.

"Do you mind if I watch?" His deep voice cut through the air.

Abby shrugged. "It doesn't matter. Everyone is going to see this anyway. They're going to think I'm horrible. I'm going to have to look for a new place to live, a place where I can start again."

That didn't sound good. He couldn't imagine what he might be about to see.

The video started. An electronic voice narrated what they were seeing.

"Some people can fool others," the narrator started.

A group of people appeared on screen. They were walking between curtains until they reached what appeared to be a dressing room area. Probably eight mirrors and tables had been set up.

A woman—someone muttered her name was Jillian—went through and opened the drawers at each of the stations.

When she looked inside the fourth one, Jillian reached into the drawer and pulled out a wad of cash.

Everyone gasped, and their gazes went to someone in the group.

Abby, Tali realized. That was Abby.

On the screen Abby's hands covered her mouth, and she shook her head. "I don't know how that got there."

"You have some explaining to do," the woman holding the money said.

"But I mean it—I didn't put that there. I'm being set up."

"Why would someone set you up?" another woman asked.

Abby looked faint in the video as she shook her head. Her gaze traveled to everyone in the crowd as the camera zoomed in on her.

"Steve, put that camera away." Jillian walked toward him and put her hand over the lens.

Then the video fast-forwarded in time. Steve—Mac could only assume—began recording again as the woman in charge led Abby to an office. Everyone around him whispered about what Abby had done.

Several minutes later, Abby exited the office, tears streaming down her face.

She grabbed her things, ran off the stage and exited the theater.

"You never know who you can trust," the narrator said, whose electronic voice was deep and slightly distorted. "Those who appear to be the most righteous around us may actually be the worst of society—someone who would steal from a charity in order to buy designer clothes for herself. Remember: a zebra doesn't change its stripes."

"Wait . . ." Mac placed his hands on his hips. "Are you saying you stole money from the last theater group you were a part of?"

Abby swung her head back and forth. "No . . . I would never do that."

"Then what exactly is happening here in this video?" Tali quietly asked the question, sounding as if she realized the delicacy of the situation.

Abby buried her face in her hands again, still a complete and utter mess.

"I was set up. By someone I cared about. And afterward, my career and reputation were ruined."

————

Tali didn't like how distraught Abby seemed about all of this.

Nor could she imagine her friend stealing anything.

Nothing about this situation made sense.

"Why don't you tell us what happened?" Cadence said in her calm, quiet voice. She leaned forward in her plush chair as they all gathered around Abby.

Abby wiped her eyes and sucked in a deep breath. "The lead actor in the play that I was in, his name was Michael . . . well, the two of us began to date. One night, I walked in on him in the office, and I saw him putting some money in his back pocket. I asked him what he was doing, and he said he was just borrowing it, and he was going to pay it back."

"That doesn't sound good," Serena muttered.

"It wasn't," Abby confirmed. "Right away, I suspected something was up. But he sounded so convincing, like what he was doing was just something normal that happened sometimes in this kind of business. I tried not to think much of it, and he asked me not to tell anybody. He said he had some debt and he just needed to pay it off, but he was going to be able to replace the money within a few days."

"What happened then?" Serena practically sat on the edge of her seat.

"The next day, Jillian noticed that the money was missing, and she called everyone together for a meeting. She knew it had to be one of us. Then she told us she was going to search the dressing rooms. When she opened the drawer beneath my makeup mirror, the money was there. Michael acted like he had no idea how it got in there. He pretended our whole conversation from the night before hadn't happened, and he looked at me as if I really had taken it myself."

"That's awful," Tali nearly gasped as she said the words.

Abby nodded before drawing in a shaky breath. "I know. I expected someone to step up to my defense. But no one did. Jillian asked me to leave. She said since she got all the money back, she wouldn't press charges, but that I was never welcome back with the theater troupe."

"Why didn't you just tell everybody that Michael

stole the money?" Mac shifted as he leaned against the wall.

"I pulled Jillian aside privately to tell her, but it didn't make any difference. She didn't believe me. She said I was trying to deflect. But Michael was always everyone's favorite. He had that kind of charming personality." Abby took a sip of her coffee, her tears tapering some.

"That's terrible." Cadence patted Abby's back. "What happened between you and Michael after that? Did he ever say anything to you about it?"

Abby swallowed hard before saying, "He played it off as if it was all my idea, and as if I totally hadn't seen him take that money. It was horrible, and I felt so betrayed, like my career was over. The theater world can be a small one, and I thought for sure that word would spread about this. It did."

"Is that why you came here to the island?" Mac asked. "Because it was far enough removed from all the other acting troupes in the area?"

Abby nodded, her skin still sickly pale. "That and because I truly do love this place. I thought maybe I could start over and prove myself."

Mac shifted. "I hate to be the one to ask this question right now, but where are all of the funds for this year's play?"

Abby blinked as if surprised by the question.

"They're in a safe in the director's office at the theater."

"We need to go check that out." Mac's shoulders visibly stiffened.

Abby quickly stood. "I didn't even think about that. But, yes, we most definitely do."

CHAPTER
SEVEN

SERENA AND CADENCE stayed at the bookstore while Tali and Mac took Abby back to the theater so she could double-check that all the money was there.

Tali knew it was simply a precaution considering the circumstances.

But she didn't like the bad feeling simmering in her gut.

The good news was that everyone had already left the theater so they shouldn't run into anybody. Tali knew that would be the last thing that Abby would want right now.

She sat in the backseat of Mac's truck with Abby as they rode there and gently rubbed her back. She knew the girl felt terrible. Tali couldn't imagine what it would have been like to go through that kind of betrayal.

On second thought, she *did* understand. When her husband had been unjustly accused of being involved in a bank robbery, she'd felt some of those same feelings.

None of them were good emotions to experience.

They arrived at the theater and climbed out. With trembling hands, Abby unlocked the door, and they slipped inside.

"Why don't you show me exactly where the cash box is?" Mac asked.

Abby flipped on just enough lights for them to see where they were walking.

Mac and Abby cut across the stage and headed toward the office, which was located behind the stage.

Tali paused for a moment on the stage and looked out at the theater.

She liked to imagine what this place was like when it was a schoolhouse. It was large—large enough to now fit a hundred seats in the audience. A small foyer was at the back, and a concession area had been set up there.

The wooden walls were rustic and weathered. The ceiling pitched high with chandelier lights there. Tali personally liked the overall look. Someone else had originally had the idea to turn this place into a theater. Quite a bit of work had been done to it before Abby bought it. The stadium-style seats had been installed. Also, a stage, catwalk, and some overhead lights had been constructed and black curtains added.

Tali turned, ready to catch up with Mac and Abby.

But she paused when she saw the set around her, all ready and waiting for the play to begin.

Her heart panged with a moment of grief.

Perhaps she had been more excited than she realized about this play. There was something special about community theater at Christmas that pulled people together. And she'd been certain this production was going to be a highlight for the island this year.

But now all that was up in the air.

As Mac and Abby reached the office, Tali paused near one of the curtains onstage.

A shattered glass ornament lay on the floor.

She was surprised someone would leave it there. Those shards were sharp. She'd broken one in her house before, and her foot had hurt for two weeks after she'd missed a small piece on the floor and had stepped on it.

Just as she bent down to clean it up before

someone got hurt, a shadow lunged from behind the curtains.

Tali gasped as strong hands hit her shoulders and shoved her to the floor.

———

Mac heard the commotion on the stage and instantly tensed.

He glanced around the office.

Tali. Where was Tali?

She had been right behind him.

He rushed from the office to the stage area.

His heart skipped a beat when he saw her lying on the floor holding her head.

He quickly sank to his knees beside her, worry rushing through him. "Are you okay?"

She sat up, her eyes scrunched and her hand still on top of her head.

"I think so . . ."

"What happened?"

"Someone pushed me down. He just ran out." She pointed her finger in the direction the person had gone.

He glanced toward the route she indicated. "Are you going to be—"

Before he could even finish his statement, Tali said, "I'll be fine. Go. See if you can catch him."

With that statement, Mac glanced at Abby, motioning for her to take care of Tali.

Then he took off.

CHAPTER
EIGHT

MAC PAUSED on the edge of the stage and surveyed the seating area in front of him. He didn't see anyone in the dark auditorium.

But the door leading outside was slightly open.

He darted in that direction.

As he stepped outside into the cool nighttime air, he paused.

It was dark out here. Dark and quiet.

Mac glanced around him, trying to figure out which direction this guy had gone.

But he saw nothing and no one.

The man hadn't just disappeared into thin air.

So where had he gone?

Mac jogged out several more steps and looked at a few houses in the distance. Some marsh grass swayed beyond that, and a few small patches of trees dotted the area.

He supposed this guy could be hiding there.

Bringing up the light on his phone, he shone it on the ground to look for prints.

But the gravel road concealed any that could have been left.

He bit back a frown.

The figure who'd run out here . . . he was gone.

———

Tali looked up when she saw Mac step back inside. Abby had helped her to her feet.

She was shaken and would most likely have a bruise, but overall she was fine.

The good news was that Mac was okay.

The bad news was that he had a disgruntled look on his face. Tali had seen that look before. It was never good.

"Mac?" She could hardly wait to hear his update even though she sensed it would be bad news.

He shook his head as he paused in front of her. "He got away."

"I'm sorry. But he had a decent head start."

"I suppose he did." Mac reached out and grasped

her face as he peered at the top of her head. "How are you?"

His voice sounded tender and laced with concern.

Tali felt a flash of warmth rush through her. "I'll be fine. Don't worry about me."

"Do I need to remind you that neither of us are as young as we used to be? Head injuries are more serious the older you get."

She waved him off again. "I know. But I'll be fine. I will."

Abby held onto the other side of her, almost as if afraid she might fall over.

Tali might be sixty-two, but she didn't feel old.

At least, she didn't until people started treating her as fragile.

"Let's get out of here. I'd feel better if we talked somewhere else." Mac ushered her and Abby to the truck.

Tali was tense as soon as she stepped outside. What if that guy was still here? If he was still hiding in the shadows?

But logically she knew that Mac had scared this person away.

Only once they were on the road did he start asking questions. "Who else has a key to this place?"

Abby shook her head. "Just me and Joe Marshall, the stage manager."

"No one else?"

"Not that I know of." Abby shrugged. "I mean, I guess the previous owner could have held onto a key to the place."

"Debbie Pennington, right?" Mac asked.

Abby nodded.

"She transformed the building from a schoolhouse to a theater and tried to make a go of the place, but it never got off the ground," Mac said.

"That's what I heard," Abby said. "She's so sweet and has been very helpful. I've asked her a million questions."

"I'm surprised she's not participating in the play then," Tali said.

"That's only because she's going to go see her son up in Maryland for Christmas. She didn't want to commit to part of it and then not be able to follow through." Abby wiped her eyes again. "I can't believe someone pushed you down, Tali. What if they'd done something worse, something that had really hurt you?"

Tali was grateful this guy hadn't. But she did want to put some ice on her head because it was already aching.

"We have a lot of things we need to figure out." Tali gritted her teeth with determination. "Let's go back to my bookstore to talk more."

CHAPTER
NINE

BY THE TIME they got back to Beach Bound Books and Beans, Cassidy had arrived. She took a statement from Tali as well as from Abby.

"What about the money?" Tali couldn't believe she'd forgotten about the cash. But with everything else that had happened, the original reason they'd gone out tonight had been shoved to the back of her mind.

"It was gone." Abby's voice cracked as she sank deeper into her chair.

Cassidy's hands went to her hips, and lines pulled across her forehead. "Wait . . . what money?"

They all exchanged glances.

Finally, Abby cleared her throat and shared the story with her.

Cassidy listened closely without any judgment in her gaze.

"So you think someone from your past came here and tried to set you up?" Cassidy clarified. "Who would be that angry with you? And exactly how much money are we talking right now?"

"We raised five thousand for Hope House." Abby's voice lifted as if that memory cheered her up some. "I was going to deposit the cash in the bank and present a check to Ty at the end of the play. I was so excited about that."

Cassidy shifted and narrowed her eyes. "Is there anyone from your past you think would do that?"

Abby let out a long breath. "Maybe Michael. He got away before with stealing that money, and he ruined my life in the process. At least, that's what it felt like. I don't know why he'd feel the need to come back here and do it all over again. I'm not sure exactly how that would help him."

Cassidy twisted her lips into a frown. "You're right. Unless there was more to the story. Maybe he purposefully wanted to set you up and ruin you. But I don't see why he would do that either. Where does this guy live anyway?"

"We were in Myrtle Beach when that fiasco happened. He could have moved on by now, but I don't keep tabs on him. With actors, a lot of times they go where the work is. His ultimate goal was to end up in New York. That's most people's goal in this industry. New York or LA."

Cassidy nodded slowly. "I'm probably going to check him out, just to make sure he's not in this area. Is there anyone else from your past that you can think of who might do this to you?"

Abby let out a sigh. "The director, Jillian, was pretty upset with me. She never believed me when I said I was innocent. I do think it's extreme, but maybe she would want to ruin me like I ruined her production. When I got the boot, she had to scramble to find another lead actor. Not to brag or anything, but I was a lot better than the person who had to step in for me. The show basically tanked."

Tali listened closely, taking mental notes on everything being said.

She'd thought that things were finally settling down.

But now it didn't appear they were.

Someone was trying to ruin Abby . . . and in the process, they might just ruin other people here on the island as well.

Tali held the ice pack on her head a little tighter at the thought.

———

Cassidy left a few minutes later.

After Tali told her goodbye, she glanced back at her book club buddies as they huddled in her cheerful coffeehouse. The only one they were missing was Tali's niece, Maisie.

Maisie had just moved to the island at the end of October and lived upstairs with Tali. However, she'd gone back home to South Carolina to wrap up a few things with her old job this week. She'd be back in a couple of days. But Tali already missed her company.

Just a couple of weeks ago, these ladies had helped her decorate for the holidays. They'd made a Christmas tree out of books and had strung lights around it. Stockings hung from shelves. Fake snow lined the picture window, and a train carrying miniature books chugged in circles around a display of books.

The place looked so festive . . . a contrast to the situation they were dealing with.

They decided they would all spend the night here tonight.

Tali still marveled that these young women in their twenties and thirties would want to hang out with someone her age. She was flattered, really.

But right now, Abby still looked distraught. Cadence tried to comfort her. Serena . . . her eyes lit as she looked at something on her phone.

Instantly, Tali's curiosity rose. She sat on the couch beside her. "Serena?"

Serena glanced at Abby and saw she and Cadence were chatting.

She showed Tali her screen.

"I've been reading the comments on that video," she said quietly.

Tali took the phone from her and pulled some reading glasses from her pocket. She began reading also.

Cancel her! Cancel her!

It's hard enough to thrive working in the arts without people stealing profits!

Worst actress ever. Her denial on this video isn't even believable.

You deserve for this to happen to you.

Lord help whoever she's surrounded herself with now.

"Ouch," Tali muttered.

Serena nodded. "Yes, ouch."

Mac finished checking all the doors and windows before coming to join them. "I'm going to run."

She stepped outside with Mac to tell him goodbye.

As they moved closer to each other, she saw that familiar tenderness in his eyes. "I'm worried about you, Goldie."

"You don't need to worry about me. I'm going to be fine."

"You always seem to find yourself in the middle of trouble. Why is that?"

Tali let out a breath. "I guess when you stand on the outside, it's easy just to skate by things on a surface level. But when you truly get involved in people's lives, you see a lot of the ugliness. That can be where the trouble comes from."

"You're right. You truly do care about people, and that's part of the reason you keep finding yourself in these situations. But I don't like it." He pushed a hair behind her ear.

Tali stepped closer, wanting to reassure him. "And I love that about you."

Mac grinned. "There are a lot of things I love about you."

She reached for his neck and wrapped her arms there. "Are there?"

Tali never thought she'd feel giddy, like a teenager in love again.

But she did. Being with Mac did something crazy and exciting to her heart.

He leaned toward her and planted a long kiss on her lips before stepping back. "Be careful tonight, and call me if you need anything. Anything at all."

"I'll do that."

As Mac stepped toward his truck, a shadow caught his eye.

Was someone out there?

Someone who was watching them?

CHAPTER
TEN

MAC SAW THE SHADOW MOVE, and his muscles instantly tensed. "Get inside and lock the door."

Then he took off.

Someone was out here.

Mac paused and glanced behind him.

Tali hurried inside the bookstore, and the ladies watched everything through the picture window.

Mac looked for the figure again.

That's when he saw the top hat. The cane. The long coat.

Wait . . . was this guy dressed like Ebeneezer Scrooge?

"Hey!" Mac called. "Wait!"

The man was fast, but Mac was faster. However, the guy dashed around the corner and out of sight.

As Mac rounded the building, he saw the island Christmas tree stretching toward the sky.

He paused.

He couldn't let this guy get away again.

But where had he gone? Was he hiding behind a display of Mary and Jesus and the shepherds and wisemen? Was he by the gingerbread village?

His guard remained up as he paced around the place, his footsteps thudding against the concrete.

Each brush of wind wound his muscles even tighter.

He felt certain that the man was still here somewhere.

The question was . . . where?

———

Tali was sure Mac wouldn't want her standing by the window if danger was close, but she couldn't help herself. She hugged Sugar to her chest as she stared outside.

All the ladies gathered around her and stared at the boardwalk also.

"Do you think he's okay?" Serena nearly sounded breathless with worry. "I could go out there and help—"

"No!" all the ladies said at once.

Things always seemed to take a turn for the worse when Serena tried to insert herself. Plus, she worked for the island's newspaper. Often, they had to clarify when they did things that it wouldn't end up tomorrow's headlines.

Usually, Serena's boyfriend, Webster, helped keep her grounded. But he was out of town this week at a conference.

"Do you think the guy who sent me that video is out there?" Abby's voice still sounded thin and frail. "I mean, at first, I just assumed whoever posted this video online did it from far away. But if someone was in the theater and if he stole the money . . . I suppose that means he's on the island. But being here seems like it would be so risky."

"You're right," Tali muttered. "It does. It's a lot of trouble for someone to go through just to get revenge on you for something that they thought you did a year ago."

"I don't like this." Abby nibbled on the bottom of her lip as she stared outside.

"Believe me," Tali said. "Neither do I."

Where was Mac? What if he was in trouble?

Tali continued to wait, but there was still no sign of movement.

If she didn't see or hear something in five minutes, she was either calling Cassidy or Tali was going out there herself.

CHAPTER
ELEVEN

"YOU KNOW I know that you're out there," Mac called.

He cringed when the words came out in a singsong manner, sung to the tune of "Do You See What I See?" The cadence didn't exactly match, but it had been close enough.

What had gotten into him?

It didn't matter.

He needed to find this guy and get some answers.

He paced around the Christmas tree with its cheerful lights and decorations. The colorful string lights around the branches cast a bright glow through the air.

Sometimes the wind was crazy cold as it came off the ocean. But not tonight. It was eerily calm out here.

During the day, this beach was blanketed with children filled with wonder and awe.

Right now, danger crackled through the air.

There were too many places this guy could hide.

He froze as a sound filled his ears.

Was that a . . . moan?

Not a moan like someone was hurt. There was something different about the sound.

Just as that thought raced through his mind, he heard another moan. Then another.

The next instant, something white floated across the side of one of the buildings before quickly disappearing.

What was happening here?

Mac's muscles remained tense and ready for action.

But first he had to figure out what kind of action might be needed here.

The white flashed again—behind him this time.

As he turned, a white blob floated beside him.

More moans filled the air.

If it didn't sound crazy, he would think he was surrounded by . . . ghosts.

Then realization hit him.

These *were* ghosts.

Not real ghosts, but some type of projections.

And they weren't just any ghosts either.

These were the ghosts of Christmas Past, Present, and Future.

He heard a footstep—a real one, not a special effect.

"Hey!" he yelled.

He started around the tree. But as he sensed movement, he looked up . . . just in time to see it crashing down toward him.

———

As Tali watched out the window, her eyes widened.

Ghosts began flying around the Christmas display.

Not ghosts like Arnie, Mark, and Jayden, who played them in the Christmas production. But they almost looked like true apparitions.

But ghosts weren't real . . .

"What in the world . . . ?" she muttered.

Mac yelled something. He started to run.

Then Ebeneezer Scrooge appeared and pushed the tree over on him.

Suddenly, Tali knew she couldn't wait any longer. Besides, the bad guy was running in the opposite direction. She should be safe.

She set Sugar back on the floor and instructed

him to stay as she rushed toward Mac—her book club members close on her heels.

On the way, Tali grabbed her phone and dialed Cassidy's number.

Cassidy promised she was on her way out to help.

Tali shoved her phone back into her pocket, and as soon as she reached the tree, she saw Mac crawling out from beneath it.

He was okay. Alive at least.

Relief filled her.

Cadence helped pull the tree the rest of the way off him.

As he stood, he picked a piece of evergreen from his thick, white hair.

He looked cranky, but okay.

"He got away," Mac announced as he wiped off his pants and scanned the area around them.

"You're my biggest concern right now." Tali frowned as she studied him, looking for any injuries.

"I should have been able to get him. But he set off those strange ghosts flying around here and distracted me. I should have known better."

"Anybody would have been distracted by those ghosts." Tali frowned at the memory of seeing them.

Tali knew *exactly* what was going on.

This was the same guy who sent Abby those

threats. The ghosts flying around the Christmas tree were the Ghosts of Christmas Past, Present, and Future.

Whoever had planned this was clever and careful.

Cadence knelt on the ground and pointed at something. "The ghosts were coming from this projector. It got turned off when the tree fell. I feel like this is something straight out of an episode of *Scooby-Doo*."

Tali tended to agree with her.

Someone had gone through a lot of trouble to hook up this projector. They could have been spotted. But apparently, that didn't matter.

The only thing that mattered was getting these threats across.

And that message basically was that Abby's sins would haunt her wherever she went.

No doubt the ghosts had been set up because this person had known they could see the apparitions from Tali's bookstore.

Tali was certain this had all been meant as a threat for Abby.

This mystery was becoming more and more perplexing by the moment.

CHAPTER
TWELVE

MAC USHERED everyone back to the bookstore. Once inside, the women fussed over him. He wasn't sure if he loved it or hated it. Maybe a little of both.

Cassidy arrived and took their statements. She'd already sent her officers out to see if they could find this Scrooge.

But Mac doubted they'd be able to.

"But what about the tree?" Cadence frowned as she stared at the massacred tree in the distance. "Shouldn't we clean that up?"

Cassidy gave her a pointed look. "You can work on that in the morning. It will be fine overnight."

That same bad feeling lingered in Mac's gut.

Whoever was behind this was determined to get their message across. Just how far would they go to do that?

"I really should head home this time." Mac let out a sigh, making it clear he hadn't had any of this on his agenda for the evening.

Then again, none of the ladies had either.

Just as before, Tali followed him outside to say goodnight.

As the two faced each other, Tali frowned. "The two of us really are a sight to see, huh?"

He couldn't help but chuckle. He plucked a silver strand of tinsel off his shirt. "We sure are." Then his gaze turned serious. "You promise to stay inside tonight?"

Tali nodded. "I will. But I don't even like thinking about what this guy might have planned next."

"That makes two of us."

Upstairs, the ladies decided to bake some Christmas cookies.

Because baking and reading always made everything better.

They'd planned on doing this before Christmas, but they'd gotten behind schedule. None of them would be able to sleep right now anyway. Their adrenaline was pumping too hard.

That's why Tali made snickerdoodles, Cadence

peanut butter blossoms, and Serena sugar cookies. Baking was a nice distraction from the heavy things happening right now in their lives. Bing Crosby crooned Christmas songs from a small speaker in the corner. Currently, he sang "White Christmas," something they had very little hope of here in Lantern Beach.

"I think we should lay out all of the suspects," Serena said as she stirred her cookie dough, flour all over her clothes, cheeks, and hair.

"I like that idea." Abby wasn't actually baking anything right now. She was only helping. She said she was too distracted to focus on mixing the proper ingredients.

This place was practically a second home for the girl, so when she reached into Tali's kitchen drawer and pulled out a spare notebook and pen, it wasn't rude or a surprise. Tali wanted the girls to feel at home.

"I guess Michael would be at the top of the list," she started. "I still find it hard to believe he'd go through all this trouble, though. But he has the theatrical experience to know how to set up that projector. He loves anything involving Dickens. And apparently, he greatly dislikes me."

Tali didn't like the sound of that. "Who else?"

"I guess we could put Joe on the list." Abby

frowned. "I don't like to think that my stage manager would be responsible for this, but he does have a key to the theater, and he was aware of how much money we had taken in through donations. We only accepted cash because we didn't have a chance to set up an online donation system yet."

"We can look into his alibi and see where he went after leaving the theater," Tali said. "It's at least worth exploring."

"I agree." Serena raised her wooden spoon and held it in the air. "There's always been something I thought was funny about Joe."

"Joe?" Cadence's eyebrows shot up. "He wouldn't hurt a fly."

"It's always the ones you least expect," Serena said with a pointed look. "That said . . . who did the videos for the play? They're kind of similar to the ones sent to you."

Abby shook her head. "It wasn't him. I asked my friend Andy Cooper to make them for me. He's a video editor up in New York. We actually went to high school together."

"Anyone else?" Tali began scooping out her dough onto a cookie sheet.

"Oh, I know!" Cadence paused and turned to look at everyone, excitement dancing in her eyes. "While I was waitressing at The Crazy Chefette, I overheard a conversation with some guy named Patrick Something or other. He was saying he'd been trying to buy the land where the theater was located for years."

Tali straightened. "Is that right?"

"But the historical society gave it a historical designation," Serena said. "That means the building can't be torn down. So he was out of luck. But you can see where someone might think it was prime real estate, especially with the popularity of Lantern Beach lately."

She wasn't sure who this Patrick guy was, but he seemed like a promising lead. "He's definitely someone we should look into then."

A couple of minutes of silence passed. The cheery Christmas music that played overhead didn't seem to do much to lighten Abby's mood—any of their moods, really.

After a moment, Abby used her finger to wipe the edge of an empty bowl and then she licked the dough from her finger. "I used to be chubby, you know."

Tali sensed she was going somewhere with this. "Is that right?"

"All through junior high and high school, I was probably thirty pounds overweight. And I never really felt like I was accepted or that people could see me for who I was because of that. It might sound like a small thing, but it didn't *feel* like a small thing. It caused a lot of insecurities in me."

"Junior high and high school have a tendency to bring out a lot of insecurities." Tali placed another scoop of dough on her cookie sheet. "Even though it's been many years since I was there, I can still remember that."

"Acting was what brought me to life," Abby continued. "Being onstage helped me find my voice and my confidence. It made me into a new person." Her face fell as bad memories seemed to hit her. "Until all of that ended."

"You can't let one person or one false accusation set you back like this." Cadence pressed a chocolate kiss on top of her warm, just-out-of-the-oven peanut butter cookies. "If you do, then the person doing this to you is going to win."

"I just don't know if anyone's going to believe in me enough to continue on with this play. They're bound to find out what happened."

"You might be surprised." Tali shrugged. "I know what it's like to have people turn against you because of a false accusation. It's hard, but you keep your chin up. And never forget the truth about yourself."

"So you guys really think that the show must go on?" Abby's gaze searched everybody in the room.

Everyone nodded enthusiastically.

Before Abby could form any words to respond, her phone buzzed. When she saw whatever was on her screen, a frown captured her entire face.

She glanced up, her face ashen again. "You guys . . . someone just sent me another video."

CHAPTER
THIRTEEN

ALL THE LADIES gathered around Abby as she sat in the chair with her phone in her hands.

"Are you sure you want us to watch this with you?" Tali glanced at Abby to be certain. "We can give you privacy if you need it."

"No, you guys have been here for me. If you would stay here with me to support me, I'd really appreciate it."

"Of course, we'll stay here with you," Cadence said. "That's what friends are for."

Tali held her breath as the video began to play.

This video was titled, "The Ghost of Christmas Present."

The video footage panned the outside of the Sandpiper Theater.

"Wait! Can you pause it?" Serena asked. "Can

anyone tell when this was filmed? It could be important."

They paused the video, looking for any telltale signs: vehicles, weather, changes to the building.

"Wait!" Abby sat up straighter. "That wreath on the door . . . I didn't put it up until four days ago!"

So this *had* been filmed recently.

The narrator's voice began, just as it did last time. "Humans are creatures of habit. They like to repeat patterns. So does Abby Mendez."

Abby sucked in a breath beside Tali, but she didn't release it.

Tali placed a hand on her back, trying to calm her.

Then the video panned to Abby counting money in her office.

Abby quickly—almost frantically—shook her head. "What? Someone was filming me? How could I not have known that?"

"Someone must have left a camera hidden somewhere," Serena muttered. "They went all out."

"And they're implying that I'm the one who stole that money." Abby swung her head back and forth again. "I didn't!"

"We believe you," Tali murmured softly.

The narrator ended with, "Lantern Beach, you've been warned. What will the Ghost of Christmas Future show you? Stay tuned."

As the video ended, Abby glanced at each of them. That same crestfallen expression captured her face. "What am I going to do?"

"We're going to get through this together," Tali said. "As soon as morning comes, we can look into our list of suspects more. If he keeps doing this, he's going to make a mistake eventually. In the meantime, you haven't seen anybody familiar here on the island, have you? Anyone from your past?"

She shook her head. "I haven't."

Tali knew one thing for sure. They need to get to the bottom of this . . . or more than the Christmas play would be ruined.

So would Abby.

———

The next morning, as Tali served the ladies homemade pancakes and fruit, Abby continued to stare at her phone.

"I keep getting texts from people about the play." She shook her head. "Most of them are just asking questions. But a few texts almost sound angry."

"Is one of those angry texts from Joe?" Cadence frowned before taking a sip of coffee and leaning back in the kitchen chair.

Abby shook her head. "Actually—no. Surprisingly enough, he hasn't tried to contact me since I didn't show up yesterday."

"That is surprising." Tali slipped a misshapen pancake to Sugar, who patiently waited at her feet for any dropped food. "Who has sent you a text? I wouldn't put it past this person to send you one."

"Arnie wanted to let me know he's praying for me," Abby said.

"That was nice of him."

"Patrick said he was sorry to hear we're having some trouble," Abby said. "He made a rather large donation to the show."

"Anyone else?" Tali asked.

"Sarah Linden—she's the woman who plays Eleanor's best friend in the play. She said she always knew she couldn't trust me. But I think she likes Joe. I've always gotten bad vibes from her."

"She's so short . . ." Tali frowned as she pictured the woman. "I don't think she fits the guy who pushed me down. He was taller."

Silence stretched for a moment.

"We're supposed to have dress rehearsal tonight." Abby set down her phone long enough to take a bite of her pancakes. "How am I going to face everybody?"

"You can't get cold feet on us." Serena raised her eyebrows in a pointed look.

"I won't," Abby insisted.

"Why don't you text the cast and crew now?" Cadence suggested as they all continued to eat. "Let them know that dress rehearsal is still a go for tonight."

Abby seemed to think about it a moment before nodding, determination hardening her gaze. "You're right. That is what I need to do."

She picked up her phone again and began to type something. A moment later, she hit a final button and put her phone down. "Done. It's sent. I also asked everyone to come a few minutes early for a quick meeting so I can explain what's happening. I'm not backing down to this bully."

"All right, everybody." Tali clapped her hands, knowing she needed to distract them from their problems for a moment. "As soon as we finish breakfast, we need to get dressed, and then we have a tree to set back up. We're not gonna let Scrooge steal this Christmas from us. Understood?"

"Yes, ma'am," Serena nodded.

Everyone else around her also nodded in agreement.

If only it could be that easy.

CHAPTER
FOURTEEN

MAC PRESSED his phone to his ear as he spoke with Cassidy and walked down the boardwalk on the way to Tali's shop.

"Okay, this Michael guy is on a break right now," Cassidy said. "He apparently went home to visit his family for the holidays, but we're still trying to confirm that."

Mac scanned the Christmas decorations around him, looking for signs of anything suspicious. Everything appeared merry and bright. He only hoped nothing sinister was hiding behind that façade.

"So he could be a suspect." Mac slowed his steps. "But I'm just not sure what motive he could have, other than just being a scumbag."

"I'm not a hundred percent sure either unless this went a lot deeper, and he simply wanted to ruin

Abby. I didn't get that indication from talking to her, but it's something worth exploring. I'm going to show his picture around the island today, maybe to some of the different property managers to see if they know anything."

"Smart thinking. What about the director? Jillian, you said. Did you look into her?"

"She's directing a show up in the DC area. They had a performance last night, and she was there, so I think we can safely rule her out."

Mac bit back a frown. "Thanks for the update, Cassidy. I appreciate all your work on this."

"No problem."

When he arrived at Tali's place, all the ladies were waiting at the door for him, already wearing their winter coats, scarves, and hats. They all looked very Christmassy and ready to face the thirty-eight-degree day.

He'd made the ladies promise not to go out without him, but he could see they were chomping at the bit.

Tali opened the door and grinned at him. "Good morning."

Just seeing her face made it seem like it would indeed be a good morning. "Hey there, ladies. You're all looking bright-eyed and bushy-tailed."

His gaze went to Abby. She also looked better

today than she did the night before. But her eyes still seemed duller than usual.

The ladies had sent him the newest video last night, the one that had been posted online about Abby.

He didn't like the way this was progressing.

They all joined him outside, even Sugar, who'd been dressed in a plaid jacket and was on a red leash.

Sometimes that dog was like a child to Tali. But Mac wasn't complaining. Sugar made Tali happy, so therefore Sugar made Mac happy.

"Let's go see if we can get this tree cleaned up and save Christmas for Lantern Beach." He said those last words with a bit of humor and drama that wasn't lost on the ladies.

They all threw him looks.

However, he needed to deflect what had happened to him last night. He didn't like being taken off guard or looking like a fool. Both of those things felt true right now.

As they walked farther down, he saw a crowd had already gathered and people were picking up ornaments. It would take a little more help to get that tree standing up again, but with the number of volunteers there, Mac knew they could do it.

He felt a rush of pride toward the people of this

island. They truly knew how to pull together when needed.

Still, he would need to be vigilant. The person who'd done this could be close. He or she could even be in this crowd, hiding in plain sight.

It was something worth keeping in mind.

As the ladies began to help pick up ornaments, Tali lingered close to him. It was probably better that way since some of the ornaments had broken. Tali had shoes on, but Sugar didn't.

As if she realized that at the same time he did, she scooped the dog up in her arms.

She turned toward Mac.

"You doing better today?" Tali didn't bother to hide the fact she was studying him.

"I'm fine. Nothing to worry about here." He rolled his shoulders back. "I've still got some resiliency left in me."

"I know, but that was quite a scare."

"As it was when that man knocked you down yesterday too."

"That did take me off guard." She frowned. "This isn't what Christmas is supposed to be about."

As he continued to scan the crowds, his gaze stopped on one person.

Joe Marshall. Stage manager. Tali had mentioned that Abby suggested him as a possible suspect. However, Mac had confirmed that when Joe left rehearsal last night, he'd gone to a friend's house, and they'd gamed for the rest of the evening.

When Joe saw Abby, he froze. Almost looked ashen.

Mac narrowed his eyes.

Joe might not be guilty, but he was hiding something, wasn't he?

————

Tali followed Mac's gaze.

He was watching Joe.

Joe stood on the sidelines observing everyone else work. The man was probably in his mid-twenties, painfully thin, and unusually pale for someone who worked at the beach.

In the summer, when tourist season was in full swing, he worked maintenance for one of the vacation property management companies here on the island. Tali wasn't sure what exactly the man did in the winter.

But, right now, Joe was definitely acting cagey with his tight shoulders and his gaze flipping back and forth between everyone.

Why was he doing that?

Would it be too bold to march over there and ask him?

"Do you think I could go strike up a casual conversation?" Tali leaned closer to Mac as she whispered the question.

"Only if I'm with you."

"If you come, he's going to clam up. Law enforcement often has the tendency to intimidate people. And Joe is easily intimidated. I see how guarded he acts around you. But I think he likes me. He said I remind him of his grandmother."

Mac narrowed his eyes. "Fine. But stay close."

Gripping Sugar, Tali made her way toward Joe, trying to look casual.

She plastered on a smile as she got closer. "Good morning, Joe."

He seemed to snap out of his stupor and pulled his gaze away from Abby for long enough to look at Tali. "Ms. Robinson . . ."

"Just call me Tali."

"Tali . . . good to see you here." He grimaced as he nodded toward the tree. "I can't believe someone pushed over the Christmas tree."

"We're all in shock." Tali wasn't sure if people knew that Mac had been under the tree when it came down, but she wasn't going to mention that. "It's nice of you to come out here and . . . help." Okay—he wasn't really helping, but she wasn't sure how else to word it.

"Whatever I can do to pitch in. I've got some spare time. It's one of the perks of being single." His gaze traveled back over to Abby.

Joe liked her, didn't he? That's why he was looking at her like that right now.

Tali let that thought sink in for a moment.

She couldn't see the two of them together. She just didn't sense any chemistry between them.

Tali needed to figure out a way to confirm her suspicion, though.

"Abby's nice, isn't she?"

Joe's gaze snapped back to Tali, more shock racing through his gaze. "Who? Abby? Oh, right. She's great. I heard that there was some stuff going on with her, and I feel for her. I really do."

"Do you think a lot of people have heard what's going on?"

He sighed. "Well, it's one of the disadvantages to small-town living, I suppose. People like having things to talk about, and other people are one of the hottest topics. They mean well. I think."

"You don't think that Abby would . . . do those things she's been accused of . . . do you?"

His face scrunched with horror. "Abby? No way. She's totally aboveboard."

"Say . . ." Tali stepped closer. "Are you dating anybody?"

Joe's cheeks reddened. "No, I'm not. Why? Are you asking me out?"

Tali's eyebrows shot up. "Me? No. I'm . . . I'm not like that."

He didn't look convinced.

That hadn't gone according to plan.

"I'm asking because I *may* know a few single young ladies here around town."

Joe's gaze went to Abby again. "I get that . . . but the one person I like would never look at me that way."

Tali shrugged. "You never know."

She wondered if his perceived rejection might make him lash out . . . and do something drastic as a means of revenge.

CHAPTER FIFTEEN

TALI LEFT Joe a few minutes later and joined Mac again as he stood on the boardwalk surveying the cleanup efforts.

"I think Joe has a crush on Abby," Tali whispered. "But he doesn't seem like the type who'd want to hurt her if the feelings were unrequited."

His eyebrows flew up. "You sure?"

"About as sure as I can be. I didn't directly ask him. Not that he would've answered if I did. But I know a man with a crush on someone when I see him."

Mac cocked his head and turned to her. "Do you? Do you see it on me, Goldie?"

Tali chuckled. "Well, you never see it for yourself when you're involved. You're not objective enough."

"I understand. This Christmas is going to be the

best one I've had for a long time." He tenderly pushed some stray hairs back from her face. "We just need to get this wrapped up so nothing gets in the way."

Tali wondered about the undertones in his voice, but she agreed. They could all stand to have a wonderful Christmas.

She'd been trying to figure out what present to get Mac. They'd only officially been dating for a little over a month and a half. Yet it felt like they had been together for a lot longer.

Still, she didn't know exactly what to get him. Cookies and sweets just didn't seem to be sufficient. A sweater, socks, or slippers seemed boring. Maybe she could track down some of the books that he liked, but that seemed so expected . . .

But she was quickly running out of time since Christmas was only a week away.

As they stood there, someone cleared her throat beside them, snapping them from their moment.

Tali looked over and saw Debbie Pennington, the former owner of the Sandpiper Theater, standing there. The stately woman was in her forties with dark hair, zebra-striped glasses, and a penchant for wearing bright pink.

"This is all horrible what's happened, isn't it?" Debbie stared at the tree.

"Debbie . . . I didn't think you were going to be in town for Christmas," Tali said. "I heard you were visiting your son."

The woman had always seemed pleasant and had frequented Beach Bound Books and Beans since it opened.

"I'm on my way to the ferry in a few minutes, but I heard what happened and wanted to stop by to see the tree for myself before I left." Debbie shook her head. "I was hoping to be here to see the play, but it didn't work out. Hopefully, the next one won't be around the holidays."

Tali pushed back a lock of hair that the wind blew in her face. "It won't be the same without you there. I know you really believe it's important to add some culture to this island."

The two had talked about it over coffee in the shop one day.

"Sometimes, things aren't meant to be, you know? You just have to accept that." Debbie's expression shifted into a frown. "I heard you guys had quite a scare yesterday at rehearsal. I'm glad everything's okay. I've always liked Abby, and I really hope she can make a go of the theater."

"That's what we're all hoping. You don't know of anyone who might want to shut down the production before it even opens, do you?"

"I was thinking about it all night, from the time I heard what happened." Debbie paused and pressed her lips together as if contemplating what she would say next. "I hate to say this, but has anyone questioned Harold Steinbach yet?"

"Harold Steinbach?" Tali mused. That was a name she hadn't expected to hear.

Harold owned Sunny Days Vacations, one of the premier vacation home management companies here on the island. The sixty-something man had a lot of influence—and a lot of money. But he was also single, and he never seemed very happy.

Abby walked up to them right as Debbie said his name. "Harold? How could I have forgotten about him? He should definitely be on the suspect list."

———

Mac listened carefully to the conversation.

He hadn't heard Harold's name pop up in a long time. But the man was peculiar and opinionated. People either loved him or hated him.

"What's Harold's beef with you?" Mac turned to face Abby, not wanting to miss any details.

Abby ran a hand over her face, that familiar sadness returning to her gaze. "I don't want to speak poorly of anyone."

"You're in safe company." Tali moved closer as if to protect her.

Still, Abby hesitated.

"He didn't want Abby to do the play," Debbie blurted.

"He's not even the artsy type," Tali said, turning to Abby. "Why didn't he want you to do the play?"

Abby frowned before saying, "He caught wind of what I was doing, that it was a retelling of the Dickens story. Then he started lecturing me about how Christmas is all about Jesus. I told him that I agreed. I thought maybe we could find some common ground. But instead, he kept lecturing me and going on and on and on about it until I felt horrible."

"He thinks there should only be religious plays at the theater?" Mac scratched his head.

"He just said he thinks anything about Christmas that doesn't focus on Jesus is wrong. I told him we could celebrate Jesus and still enjoy the holidays in other ways. I mean, I love Jesus too. But Mr. Steinbach made me feel like such a horrible person. He told me he was going to get the production shut down."

"What?" Mac's voice rose. "Then why isn't he trying to get the Christmas tree taken down? Or the life-size gingerbread houses?"

"Somebody *did* knock the tree down last night," Tali reminded him.

"Point taken." He shrugged and cast her a wry expression.

"It doesn't make sense, though," Tali said. "You do have a nativity in your play."

Abby let out a long, almost burdened breath. "The truth is that I thought about what he said, and I realized I would like to incorporate some of the real Christmas story into my play. That's when I decided to do dual timelines with the nativity on one side and a modern-day Dickens on the other. Most of all, I hoped to get a greater message across—the reality that hearts can be changed and love always wins."

Mac and Tali exchanged a look.

"I think we need to go talk to Harold," Tali muttered.

Mac nodded. "I agree."

————

Mac, Tali, Sugar, and Abby headed in Mac's truck toward Harold's place. It was one of the nicer homes on the island, with baby-blue siding, multiple decks all trimmed in a crisp white, and a distinctive craftsman look.

Tali could call Cassidy but, according to Mac, she

was in the middle of mediating a neighborly feud about Christmas lights.

Finally, they pulled up to Harold's cottage. Mac put the truck in Park, and they all climbed out.

Tali had met Harold before, and she didn't think he was the violent type. Then again, she didn't think he was the religious type either. There was only one church on the island, and she'd never seen him there. Not that he couldn't worship from home. But still . . . something about it all felt a little off.

Mac took the lead as they walked toward the front of Harold's house.

But when they reached it, they saw that the door was open.

It was thirty degrees outside today and windy—not the kind of day people usually left their doors open for some fresh breeze to get inside.

Especially without a storm door.

A bad feeling brewed in Tali's stomach as she wondered what they would find inside.

CHAPTER
SIXTEEN

MAC DIDN'T LIKE THIS.

He'd been in too many similar situations before.

Most of them didn't turn out well.

He drew his gun and called into the house, "Harold? Are you here?"

There was no answer.

Mac scanned the place.

His gaze stopped on the man's Christmas tree.

Wait . . . Harold had a tree? Mac thought he didn't believe in those types of Christmas displays.

He stored that tidbit away as he crept farther into the space.

The living room was clear.

So was the kitchen.

Tali, Abby, and Sugar waited at the door for him as he continued into the hallway toward the two bedrooms on this level. Mac had been to Harold's place for a few parties in the past. Harold had hosted each of them in an effort to influence others. The man, though cranky, could turn on the charm when he wanted.

The first bedroom—which appeared to be a guest bedroom—was empty.

But when he opened the door to the second bedroom, he spotted someone sprawled on the floor.

Harold.

Mac's heart pounded harder.

Was he unconscious . . . or was he dead?

———

Within minutes, Cassidy arrived at the scene as well as paramedics.

Tali stood outside with Abby, hugging Sugar to her chest with one hand and with the other, she covered her mouth so no one could see how it dropped open in horror.

As the paramedics took Harold away on a stretcher, she couldn't help but feel unsettled.

Mac had been talking to Cassidy, but now he wandered back toward Tali and squeezed her hand. "I'm sorry you had to see that."

"What do you think happened to him?"

"There was a lamp on the floor beside the bed." Mac frowned. "Based on the blood on it, it looks as if maybe someone hit him."

"But he's alive?" Tali asked.

Mac nodded. "Yes, but in critical condition."

"Do you think this is related to everything else going on with the theater?"

Mac shrugged, but the motion looked heavy and burdened. "It's hard to say."

Tali let out a sigh. "I just don't know what's going on in this town. Is there ever a moment of peace?"

A soft smile tried to curl the side of his lips. "Sometimes. I promise. It's not always like this here."

Tali hoped that was the truth. Because she loved this island . . . but she didn't love coming face-to-face with death and danger so often.

CHAPTER
SEVENTEEN

MAC DROPPED TALI, Sugar, and Abby off at the bookstore and headed out. Serena and Cadence were waiting for them there when they arrived, anxious to hear anything new.

They barely made it out of the entryway downstairs before Abby began to talk and give them an update.

"It has to be Michael." Abby wrapped her arms over her chest as she paced the bookstore. "He's the only one that makes sense."

"We know he is not in a play right now." Tali put some water into a bowl for Sugar and placed it on the floor. The dog thirstily lapped it up. "But we don't know where he is."

"I could call his sister." Abby's eyes suddenly lit.

"His sister?" Tali repeated. In her mind, this had bad idea written all over it. But maybe she was over-thinking it.

"Krissy has always loved me, even after Michael and I broke up. She was one of the few people who said she didn't believe what others were saying about me and that Michael had been a fool to break up with me."

"Do you think she would talk to you if you called?"

"I think she might. With so much being on the line right now, it seems like it should be worth a try, right?"

"If you're comfortable doing it, then go for it," Tali said.

Abby drew in a shaky breath, hesitating only a moment before dialing the number. She put the phone on speaker so everyone could listen.

The phone rang once. Twice. Three times.

All this anticipation, and no one was going to answer, were they? That would fit their luck, unfor-tunately.

Then, on the fifth ring, a soft voice came over the line. "Is this really you, Abby?" Friendliness tinged the woman's tone.

Abby straightened. "It's me, Krissy. How are you?"

"I can't tell you how happy I am to hear from you! I've been thinking about you lately and wondering how you're doing."

"I'm doing just fine."

"Michael said you moved to some small island. Lantern Beach or something."

Tali sucked in a breath. So Michael *did* know where Abby was. That could work against him right now.

"That's right. I'm trying to get a small theater started here. I thought it could be a good change of pace."

"Will you let me know about any shows you have after the holidays? I'm gonna do everything I can to be there and watch it. Okay?"

"That sounds great, Krissy."

The two made a few more minutes of small talk.

Then Abby's gaze flickered around nervously. Tali could tell she wasn't thrilled about where this conversation would go next. But she'd come this far and, if Tali had to guess, Abby wasn't going to stop now.

"Say, I know Michael and I broke up," she started. "But I don't like to live with hard feelings. How's he doing?"

"Overall, he's fine. But he's not spending Christmas with us this year. Can you believe it?"

"What? No, I can't believe that. Where is he spending it if he's not with you guys?"

"I don't know. He didn't tell us. He just said that he and his friends were going to spend it together. But I know for a fact that all of his closest friends are going to be with their families. I don't know if he made some new friends or what. But none of us are very happy with him."

Tali let that fact settle in her mind.

Yes, Michael was definitely moving up on her suspect list.

———

After Mac dropped the ladies off at the bookstore, he decided to stroll over and check the progress of the Christmas tree.

It was partially his responsibility as mayor anyway, he figured.

As he ambled down the boardwalk, he reached into his jacket pocket and fingered the jewelry box there.

He rubbed his fingers against the velvet covering.

Tucked inside was an engagement ring.

He knew it was too soon to propose. All his logic told him that.

But he also knew that when you found the right one, you knew it. Besides, he wasn't getting any younger. Carol, his first wife, had been a wonderful woman, but she'd been gone for a long time now.

He wanted to spend the rest of his life with Tali. He knew that as sure as he knew the sun rose every morning.

He had a few ideas about how he might want to propose, but nothing was set in stone yet. He wanted it to be possibly spontaneous, and he figured when he knew the moment was right, that's when he would do it.

But this newest mystery might throw all of his plans into a tailspin. Tali probably wasn't even thinking about her future, not in the midst of her friend suffering as she was.

He pulled his hand from his pocket, leaving the jewelry box there for now.

He paused near the Christmas display and glanced up at the tree.

It had been raised from the ground and stood proudly illuminating the area now, almost as if nothing had happened.

"That's an impressive tree."

Mac looked over and saw Patrick Graham standing there. The man was in his fifties and tall with a bright white smile and surprisingly wrinkled skin. Then again, he'd been a surfer when he was younger and he spent a lot of time in the sun. Today, he was a real estate developer.

He seemed nice enough, but not the kind of guy Mac would want to spend a lot of time with. He was too into appearances and business.

"It really is a nice tree."

"You're doing a good job running this town, Mac. I know it's a lot sometimes."

Mac chuckled. "I can't argue with that."

"I'm afraid all these crimes are going to drive tourists away, however. They seem to come in waves."

"It's true." Mac rubbed his jaw, feeling a tightness there. "But we're doing everything we can to keep people safe. I can promise you that."

"I hope that's true. Because there's a lot riding on the tourism of this town."

Mac didn't like the man's tone. Were there subtle undertones of a threat to his statement?

Before they could talk more, sirens roared in the distance.

Mac's shoulders tightened.

That sounded like the fire department and the police.

As if reading his mind, his phone rang. It was Cassidy.

"You'll never believe this," she started. "But Abby's duplex is on fire."

CHAPTER
EIGHTEEN

TALI HELD Abby's hand as they rushed toward her house in Mac's truck.

She couldn't believe what Mac had told her.

It almost seemed like a bad dream. She knew it wasn't. She could still hear the sirens. Still smell a burning scent. Still see the black flume of smoke rising in the air in the distance.

Abby, usually such a talker, was now quiet beside Tali, almost as if she couldn't even comprehend what was happening.

"Do you have a mortgage on this place?" Mac called over his shoulder.

"I'm renting it. I'm assuming the police will let the owners know what happened."

"They will," Mac said. "Did you have a lot of valuables inside?"

"I like to travel light. I have some pictures, I suppose. But they're all backed up on a Cloud drive so I should be able to get them. Other than that it's just clothes and things of that sort mostly. My laptop also. Thankfully, my neighbor is spending the winter in Florida."

They parked farther down the street because of all the emergency vehicles. As they climbed out, Tali saw several neighbors standing in their yards watching the destruction take place.

Tali could understand. It was hard to take her eyes off of the flames devouring the duplex.

Abby's breath caught when she saw the charred walls and missing roof.

Her house was a total loss. Even Tali knew that, and she didn't know about these things in general.

The walls were all black. The roof was completely gone.

"Someone had to use some kind of accelerant to make it happen like this." Mac rubbed his jaw. "There's no way this place went up this quickly on its own. There's no chance you left an iron on or anything else, right?"

Abby shook her head. "I didn't."

"Oh, Tali . . ." Abby muttered and sniffled.

Tali put her arms around the girl and let her cry into her shoulder.

This was *not* the Christmas wish that Abby was looking for.

No one wanted something like this to happen.

No one but the person responsible for it.

———

As Mac watched the firefighters put out the rest of the flames, unrest jostled inside him.

He hadn't heard an official word on this, but his gut told him that the same person who'd sent Abby those videos was the person who'd done this to her house.

Someone was very determined to send her a message.

And they'd done just that.

But this person's behavior was clearly escalating. So what would they do next?

Part of him didn't even want to think about it.

The fire chief came over to ask Abby a few questions.

She seemed to be handling things as well as could be expected. Tali stood beside her, helping her remain upright.

Mac stayed close just in case they needed anything.

As the moments went by, he glanced at his watch.

There were only six hours until dress rehearsal.

But why did that countdown feel more like a ticking time bomb that was about to explode?

CHAPTER
NINETEEN

"THERE'S nothing else we can do here for now. They'll call us if they need us, right?" Tali glanced at Mac for confirmation.

Mac nodded. "I'm sure they will. We'll probably want to grab a bite to eat now since we have rehearsal coming up this evening."

"Sounds good." Tali coaxed Abby away from the scene and into the truck.

They went to The Crazy Chefette, one of Abby's favorite restaurants, and found a seat at their favorite booth. It was one in the back of the place, where they could see everything.

Tali only liked sitting here because Mac did. He liked to be aware of what was going on around him at all times. It was just one more thing that she loved about him.

Tali slid in beside Abby while Mac sat across from them.

They each ordered one of Lisa's famous grilled cheese and peach sandwiches, along with homemade chips.

Comfort food was definitely in order for all of them. The cheery sounds of "Rocking Around the Christmas Tree" sounded overhead, the melody desperately trying to push away their blues.

"So, Harold's not behind this." Abby swirled her straw in her glass of sweet tea. "Then who is?"

"I guess Michael is still on the table, right?" Tali said. "No one knows where he is."

"Or there's always Joe," Mac added.

Abby frowned. "Joe? He seems so innocent. I can't imagine him doing this."

"Or there's Patrick Graham," Mac reminded them. "He wants that property so he can develop some condos. He said there's a lot of money at stake here. And he's afraid some of the recent crimes on the island might drive people away."

As they all chewed on that, Abby's phone buzzed.

Tali knew by the way her face went pale exactly what she had gotten.

It was the third and final video.

The Ghost of Christmas Future.

———

"Can we watch it with you?" Tali asked Abby.

Abby nodded, even though the motion looked shaky.

Mac slid into the booth beside them and leaned closer so he could also see.

This video started differently than the rest—probably because there wasn't any footage of Abby's future. Instead, the sender had to get creative.

There was another picture of the theater. But this time, the image was split in half.

"People don't change," the narrator said. "Do you see the ruin you're going to bring to this island? The theater will suffer the same way in the future as it did in the past."

Abby gasped, her hand pressed over her mouth.

Then more images filled the screen. Images of people crying. Of a *Closed* sign on a generic door. An image of Hope House, only the filter was gray and bleak.

"You did this, Abby Mendez. You! You never escape your past. Don't you know that?"

Then the video ended, leaving them all reeling with shock.

CHAPTER
TWENTY

MAC WATCHED from across the table—he'd moved back to his original seat—as Tali tried to cheer Abby up.

But the girl was clearly devastated. Whoever was sending these messages was simply vicious. And they apparently had too much time on their hands as well. These videos had taken some time and skill to create, and someone had been determined to perfectly execute every step of this situation.

He stored that fact in the back of his mind.

What would this person do next? Would they only stop sending these videos once Abby left the island and the theater shut down? Was that their goal?

But now all three ghosts had told their Christmas stories. So what was left to do even?

The question seemed to haunt him for a moment.

Then from across the table, Tali brightened. "I have an idea."

"Go on," Mac said, curious about where she was going with this.

"I keep thinking about what was said at the end of that last video. The theater was supposed to suffer the same fate in the future as it did in the past."

"What about it?" Mac asked.

"So, what happened to it back in the past?"

He shrugged, trying to think through everything he knew about the place.

"It was built back in the 1920s." Mac gave Abby a pointed look. "And in case you're wondering, that was before my time."

Abby shrugged but didn't deny that she may have thought it.

"Of course, it was a schoolhouse when it was built. It had been closed for decades, and then Debbie bought it and tried to turn it into a theater, but she couldn't get all the funding for it, so it eventually folded. Then, thankfully, the historical society stepped in and gave Abby the grant so she could reopen it."

"There has to be something more." Tali tapped her fingers on the table. "I want to look into the history of the place."

"And how do you propose we do that?" Mac asked.

Tali grinned. "The library, of course."

––––––––

As soon as they got to the small library, Tali found Gretchen, the librarian. The woman was in her eighties and could barely walk or see. But she'd been taking care of this library for fifty years and she had no plans of giving it up.

The woman was slight, with thick glasses due to her glaucoma. Tali had always enjoyed talking to her. However, the woman was not open to any ideas Tali might have on how to revitalize this place.

It had dwindled down until it was just one room full of mostly nonfiction and research books. Libraries were hard to come by in beach towns that relied on tourism.

"How can I help you?" Gretchen asked.

"I need to find some information about the old schoolhouse where the theater is. I was hoping that you could help."

"I might be able to do that," she said, her voice frail and slow. "I have some articles about it."

Tali's heart quickened. "You do?"

She waved her cane in the air in a circular motion. "Sure do. Follow me."

The three of them followed her through the library and into a door at the back. In the center of the space was a table with two large machines.

A grin stretched across Tali's face. Microfiche.

"What's that?" Abby asked.

"Way back before there was the internet, people researched by looking on microfiche."

"And what exactly is that?" Abby asked, still looking confused.

"Microfiche is what we used to use to find out information before the internet took over," Tali explained. "Documents were photographed and shrunk in size. Then they were placed on these sheets where they have to be magnified in order to read them. You have to use a card system in order to find out where to look for the information you need."

"Do you know how to find the topics that you're looking for?" Gretchen pushed her glasses up higher on her face as she hunched over her cane, looking like she needed to sit down.

"I sure do," Tali said.

She rubbed her hands together. She was in her element right now. Even the smell of the library made her excited.

Now it was time to dig in.

CHAPTER
TWENTY-ONE

AN HOUR LATER, Tali thought she had found something that could be useful. Mac and Abby sat on either side of her, and she knew they were running out of time. Dress rehearsal was slated to begin soon —in only two and a half hours.

But they were so close right now to finding out some information.

Apparently, as far back as when the island was founded, they had had some sort of newspaper. And most of those issues had been documented and preserved here on microfiche.

Tali had narrowed it down to any articles about the schoolhouse turned theater. They went through several about the place until finally stopping on a couple of more recent ones.

One was from when the theater had changed

from a schoolhouse into the theater. Later articles talked about how the historical society had stepped in to designate the building as a historical place here on the island.

Debbie had been quoted and said how excited she was about the possibility of opening the theater. She'd hoped someone else would carry on her vision.

Tali felt badly for the woman that it hadn't worked out, but she was glad the place had another chance. She didn't want to see that ruined.

Then she checked out the other article, this one about developer Patrick Graham.

"Patrick said, 'This is prime real estate,'" Tali read aloud. "'It's a shame to see it sitting here untouched. I believe the historical society only made this recent designation simply as a personal attack against me. One of the members dislikes me after I legally purchased her family's land and built four houses there. Personal vendettas have no place in the island's policies.'"

They all looked at each other.

"I just keep going back to Patrick again and again." Tali leaned back in her chair and let out a breath. "He seems to have the best motive here. He wants that land, so why not try to drive Abby away so he can maybe get his hands on it?"

Mac tilted his head to the side. "You may be onto

something. Maybe we should check him out a bit more."

––––––––

Mac had always liked Patrick. He didn't want to think of the man as being capable of doing something like this. And there was the fact that Patrick wasn't exactly handy when it came to technology. Sure, he was a savvy businessman. But could Mac really see him putting together those videos?

Not really.

But he agreed with Tali when she said that he probably had the best motive.

They began to put all of the microfiche away and return the room to the state in which they found it. He knew that Abby needed to get to rehearsal soon.

"Can you guys really see Patrick dressing up like Ebeneezer and going out in public in order to push that tree over on me?" Mac voiced his question aloud.

Tali and Abby paused near the door of the room and looked at him.

"You'd probably be surprised what some people would do to get what they want," Tali said. "You've seen things like that, right?"

His jaw hardened. "I have. But that's awfully

risky for Patrick. I'm not sure I can see him taking it that far."

"So you don't think it's him?"

He shrugged. "I'm not sure. There's something that still isn't quite clicking in place for me."

Before he could develop that thought any more, Abby's phone rang. She glanced at the screen. "It's Joe. He was supposed to get there early to get things set up for me. Excuse me one minute."

Abby put the phone to her ear and said several things. But instantly, he sensed something else was off.

"What now?"

He should learn not to ask that question, however.

Because when she ended the call and lowered her phone, she announced, "Someone vandalized the theater. I don't know if there's any way we're going to be ready to open the doors tomorrow night."

CHAPTER
TWENTY-TWO

FIFTEEN MINUTES LATER, they arrived at the theater.

Tali, Mac, and Abby stood onstage and surveyed the damage.

Red spray paint streaked along the walls. No messages had been left—just wavy, sloppy lines of paint. The concession stand at the back of the room had been knocked over, and the snacks and drinks lay scattered in disarray. The Christmas tree near the door had been ripped apart.

The scenery had taken the majority of the damage. The backdrops had been torn in half. Furniture had been smashed. Some pillows had been shredded, and their stuffing was strewn everywhere —including between the seats in the audience.

"This is it." Abby shook her head, defeat in her voice. "The show is off."

"We can clean it up." Tali patted her back again.

"If we clean this up, then we're not going to have time to rehearse." Abby raked a hand through her hair. "And what about the scenery and props? They're all ruined. What would we use? We can't recreate these backdrops in time."

"We could try the play without any props." Tali shrugged, feeling like her idea was lame. "Or we could throw something else together. We can't give up yet."

Abby turned to her. "Do you really think we can still pull this together? Look at all this destruction."

Before Tali could answer, the doors at the back of the auditorium opened, and people flooded inside. Not just the cast and crew members either. Apparently, word had spread throughout town about what happened here.

If there was one thing that residents of Lantern Beach were good at doing, it was showing up when they were needed. That was evident when the Christmas tree had fallen over, and everyone had pitched in to clean it up. And that was just one example. They'd also helped Tali get her bookshop in order and ready to open.

Tali smiled. That community care and concern was evident right now also.

Because everyone who'd come was carrying mops and buckets and the tools needed to straighten this place up and get it ready in time for opening night.

Ty Chambers stood at the forefront of the group, acting as their fearless leader with a toolbelt around his waist and a drill in his hands.

"We're here for you, Abby," he told her. "We're gonna get this place back up and running. You should be able to start your dress rehearsal on time. But we've got to get busy."

———

As Mac worked on repairing the concession stand, he also kept an eye on everything, trying to ensure no other trouble came this way.

He prayed it wouldn't, yet he knew this ordeal was far from being over . . . unfortunately.

However, exactly an hour after everyone had arrived, the theater had been cleaned and straightened. The spray paint had been scrubbed from the walls. The concession stand had been fixed and restocked. The Christmas tree was replaced.

It wasn't as good as new, but it would definitely

work. No permanent damage had been done to the structure itself. But they still had the issue of the scenery and props to deal with. He'd heard some of the ladies behind him on the stage talking about it.

With tears in her eyes, Abby thanked everyone, and then the volunteer crew cleared out so dress rehearsal could begin.

Right as they did, the remaining cast and crew showed up.

Everyone sat in the audience while Abby nervously stood on the stage and gave them an update. She told them about the videos. About what had happened back in Myrtle Beach. About what had happened over the past couple of days.

Then she begged for their trust and for them to give her another chance.

She was transparent and held nothing back.

When she finished, she waited for their reaction.

Mac held his breath as he waited to hear their response. He hoped everything didn't go downhill now.

"We stand behind you." Arnie stepped forward to show his support.

Then someone else moved up beside him. "I second that."

Before Mac knew it, each cast and crew member had agreed.

With every positive affirmation, Abby's face seemed to brighten.

"Thank you all so much for believing in me." Abby nearly sounded breathless as she said the words. "I won't let you down. I'll prove to you that I'm someone you can trust. But for now, we all need to get in costume. We need to get this practice going."

As everyone scattered, Mac's gaze went to the back of the auditorium again.

Someone else had just stepped inside.

Patrick Graham.

What was he doing here?

Mac bristled.

Because Mac considered him a suspect . . . and he hoped the man hadn't come under the guise of being concerned to check out the damage he'd done to the place.

CHAPTER
TWENTY-THREE

TALI FOLLOWED Mac's gaze and saw Patrick standing at the back of the theater.

As Mac started toward the man, she quickly caught up.

She wasn't sure if she was trying to keep a rein on Mac—what would be an impossible, useless task—or if she wanted to hear what exactly this guy had to say.

Maybe both.

Why would he be here right now? He never showed any interest in this play before—except for that large donation he'd made.

Which was kind of suspect.

Had he done so as a smokescreen? To make sure no one got suspicious?

She read enough mystery novels to know that the

smartest criminals were experts at covering their crimes. But they always made some kind of fatal mistake.

"What brings you by here?" Mac perched his hands on his hips as he stopped in front of Patrick.

"I got a note saying I was supposed to show up." He glanced around as if confused.

"Who sent you the note?" Tali narrowed her eyes with thought.

"I wish I knew. But I have no idea. They said there was going to be a surprise for me here."

Tali contemplated Patrick's words. Was he telling the truth? Did someone lure him here? Or had he made up that excuse to justify his presence?

She couldn't be sure.

"Did you bring the note with you?" Mac asked. "I'd like to see it."

"Sorry. Didn't think I needed it, so I tossed it in the trash."

Mac's eyes narrowed.

That seemed awfully convenient, Tali mused.

Patrick glanced at the stage, where Abby stood directing people on what needed to be done before practice started.

Cadence had put together a beautiful backdrop consisting of strands of jute dotted with blue and yellow paper stars. The rips in the furniture had been covered with Christmas-themed blankets and pillows. A table with a broken leg had been repaired.

At least, the screen hadn't been ripped. If it had been left down, it probably would have been. Thankfully, it had been secure—as had the projector located in the sound booth above. A lock had been installed on the door leading to it.

Tali knew she should be getting dressed. She needed to get into her angel costume so they could begin practice soon. But this felt important.

"It would be a shame if this theater shut down, wouldn't it?" Mac eyed Patrick as he said the words.

"What are you implying?" Patrick narrowed his gaze.

Before Mac could reply, a snap suddenly cracked through the air.

In the blink of an eye, one of the lights above the stage broke loose and began crashing to the floor.

Directly overtop of Joe.

———

Mac rushed to the stage just after the heavy light smashed down. He got there at the same time as Cassidy.

"Are you okay?" Cassidy rushed, kneeling beside Joe.

Joe held his leg, but there was no blood. He must have dived out of the way at the last moment.

"Yeah. I'm okay. That was close," Joe muttered.

Ty Chambers helped him to his feet. It took a moment, but Joe was able to put some weight on his leg.

But that could have been so much worse.

Mac glanced up at the catwalk above them. "How did the light fall like that?"

"There's no reason it should have fallen." Abby's voice cracked, and she rubbed her throat. "Unless someone sabotaged it."

Mac didn't see anyone on the narrow catwalk above. "Someone could have set this up earlier, and it just happened to fall now when it did."

Cassidy frowned. "That would fit everything else that seemed to be going on."

Abby ran a hand over her face. "I just can't catch a break."

"Is it even safe for us to be here?" Sarah Linden asked, an accusatory tone to her voice.

Mac wanted to give everyone the reassurance that the theater was secure. But he couldn't do that. Not in good faith, at least.

"Should I cancel this rehearsal?" Abby's question hung in the air, not directed at anyone in particular.

Instead, her gaze scanned everyone around her as if looking for an answer.

Finally, Joe stepped forward. "No, we need to keep going. This person can't get what they want. They can't win."

Tali nodded. "I agree. We all need to keep our eyes open. But we need to do this."

Abby's gaze went to Cassidy.

Cassidy shrugged. "It's fine with me if we continue. We just need to be vigilant."

Abby nodded and let out a long breath. "Okay then. We're not going to let the person behind this win. If you see something, say something. In the meantime, let's get started."

CHAPTER
TWENTY-FOUR

TALI HAD DONNED her angel costume, but she wasn't exactly feeling angelic. No, if she got her hands on the person behind these acts . . . she'd have plenty of not-so-nice things to say.

Her mind couldn't stop racing over everything that had happened.

She was on edge—as was everyone at dress rehearsal.

How had the person behind all of this been sure that that light would fall when someone was here? How had they been hiding inside the theater that day when Tali had been shoved to the floor? And how had they escaped so fast without leaving any signs of where they'd gone?

It didn't make sense. What were they all missing?

She tried to focus on practice and not miss any of

her cues. But it was challenging to concentrate on the play with everything that had happened.

As the house lights were lowered and the projector came on, Tali watched, waiting for the first video to fill the screen.

But the video that played wasn't the one Abby had created for this play.

This was the video that had been sent to Abby, the one where her castmates had accused her of stealing that money.

Everyone around her gasped and began murmuring amongst themselves. Abby ran a hand over her face, obviously struggling to know how to react. Mac straightened, his protective instincts kicking in.

Someone had sabotaged the play . . . again.

The sound guy quickly cut the video, but tension crackled in the air.

"I can still pull up the right video," the sound guy said. "I don't know what happened . . ."

Tali did.

This was just one more part of someone's evil plan to destroy Abby.

But this person couldn't have known that Abby would tell everyone beforehand what she'd been accused of. Hopefully, that would soften the blow to Abby.

As Tali glanced at the back of the stage area, a shadow moved.

Her breath caught.

Was the bad guy here?

She had a feeling he was.

She couldn't let this guy get away with this again.

"Mac! Cassidy!" She nodded toward the back of the stage.

Then they all took off toward the movement.

———

Had Tali seen something he hadn't?

Mac and Cassidy easily caught up with her as she darted behind the stage, down several steps, and into the office area.

But the hallway was empty.

"Tali?" Mac paused near the office and glanced around.

She frowned, but that determined look remained in her gaze. "I know I saw somebody back here. I'm sure of it."

"Could you make out any details?" Cassidy asked.

"Unfortunately, no." Tali let out a breath. "I think whoever it was wore all black."

Mac didn't even believe in ghosts. But whoever this was seemed to be walking through walls.

"Tali?" someone said behind them.

They turned toward the sound. Serena stood there.

"Someone from City Hall dropped this off for you." Serena handed Tali something. "I thought you'd want to see this. I believe you asked for the blueprints of this place one day last week."

"That's right." Tali nodded. "I did."

"You wanted the blueprints?" Mac turned to her, not bothering to hide his confusion.

"I thought it might help Abby in case she wanted to do any more renovations in the future. I almost forgot I requested them, however. I definitely didn't expect to get them now."

Tali opened the tube and spread it out on the floor in front of them.

They stared at the design for several moments before Tali sucked in a breath. She pointed to a spot on the stage. "Right here."

"What's there?" Mac asked.

"It's a trap door so people can move props in and out," she explained. "There are a couple on the stage we already know about, but this old one must have been concealed. But someone knew it was there.

That's how they've been able to move in and out of this space so easily."

"Where is it exactly?" Mac asked.

Tali rose and glanced around the dark space.

Then she pointed to an area of the wall that had wood paneling, probably six feet away. "Right there."

CHAPTER
TWENTY-FIVE

TALI REACHED FOR THE WALL, but Mac pushed himself in front of her.

"Let me," he muttered.

He glanced at Cassidy for approval, and she nodded.

Mac pressed on the panel.

The section was spring-loaded and popped open.

As it did, something stirred inside.

A shadow.

This was definitely where that person had gone.

Where the person still was.

"Stop right there!" Mac yelled before darting into the narrow space.

Slinking down to accommodate the five-foot-high space, he paused inside as darkness surrounded him.

The last thing he needed was for someone to surprise him.

He pulled up the flashlight on his phone and shone it around him.

As he did, someone in a black robe disappeared in the distance.

"Hey!" Mac yelled, knowing his command was futile.

When did criminals ever actually stop when they were told to?

Mac ducked around the corner in the tight space.

When he did, he saw the person who'd been back here was now trapped at a dead end.

There was nowhere else for him to go.

"You might as well just give this up." Mac was aware of the gun beneath his robe, but he didn't want to pull it out. Too much could go wrong in this small space. But the person had shown dangerous tendencies. He needed to be careful.

Finally, the robed figure slowly turned around.

As their face came into view, Mac squinted in surprise.

This was the last person Mac had been expecting to see.

———

As Tali anxiously waited for Mac to reappear, her thoughts raced.

There was only one person she could think of who would know about this trap door.

One person who might be bitter because Abby had gotten the grant from the historical society, which had allowed her to open this place back up and give it another shot.

It just so happened that this person also was adept in graphic design and video editing. In fact, this person worked for Harold Steinbach at times doing videos and graphics for his property management group.

Mac stepped out—appearing unharmed—clutching someone's arm as he pulled them into the hallway.

Tali held her breath as she waited.

The black robe the person wore made it almost impossible to make out any features.

But when Mac pulled the hood down, Tali wasn't surprised at the person she saw.

Debbie Pennington.

Her stately figure was broad enough that she could pass for a man. Plus, she knew how to do makeup and disguise her appearance.

Everything made sense.

"Debbie?" Abby gasped, her hand flying over her heart.

Debbie scowled and looked away, not saying a word.

"How could you do this to me?" Abby asked. "You told me you wanted to see this place succeed."

"I wanted to see it succeed on my terms." Debbie sneered. "The historical society didn't try to do *me* any favors. When I ran out of money, I was just out of luck. But then you waltz onto the island, and they suddenly give you a substantial sum of money to fix this place up—this place that was *my* dream? It wasn't right."

"So you tried to destroy Abby's reputation?" Tali asked.

A flash of shame swept through Debbie's gaze. "Sure, I was trying to drive her away. I thought that maybe I could step in and take over if she left. But it didn't seem like anything was going to scare her off —not with all of you supporting her. I had no idea you'd all surround her like troops going into battle."

"That's what friends do." Tali looped her arm through Abby's.

"How did you even find those videos of me?" Abby asked.

Debbie shrugged. "I have connections in the acting world. One of them just so happened to be the person who was doing the documentary. We started talking and one thing led to another. As soon as I saw the videos . . ." She shrugged again.

"I can't believe that you'd do this," Tali muttered. "I thought you were better than this."

Tali really couldn't believe it.

"How could you do this to Harold?" Cassidy asked as she pulled out handcuffs. "You've worked for him for a long time. You could have killed him."

More shame filled her eyes. "After I took that money from the safe here, he saw me leaving. He was coming here to give Abby a piece of his mind. Do you know how much he hates the idea of what you were doing?"

"He made that clear," Abby muttered.

"After the news leaked in town that money was missing from the theater, I figured he might put things together, so I went over to have a talk with him," Debbie continued. "But he got accusatory. He wouldn't listen to me. I didn't mean to hurt him. I really didn't. All I could think about was getting him to be quiet. That's why I picked up that lamp and swung it at him." Debbie shook her head, her face crestfallen. "I never meant for anyone to really get hurt."

"Yet you let a light fall from the ceiling?" Mac sounded skeptical.

"That wasn't me. I really think that may have just been an accident. I don't like heights, so I didn't go up on the catwalk."

Tali didn't know whether that was the truth or not.

"Did you set the fire at Abby's place?" she asked.

Based on the guilty expression on Debbie's face, Tali would guess the answer was yes.

"I knew she wasn't home," Debbie finally said. "She wouldn't be hurt. But I thought it might drive her off the island, at least. Then I could take over the theater again and give up this lousy graphic design job."

"What about Patrick?" Mac asked. "I'm assuming you sent that note asking him to come here."

"I . . . I just got nervous. I thought if he showed up here tonight, that maybe his presence would deflect from me. After all, he gave me such a hard time when I purchased this place. I figured he deserved a little scrutiny."

The good news was that this all seemed to be over.

"Debbie Pennington, you're under arrest for . . ." Cassidy started.

The show might actually go on, Tali realized. Maybe everyone could finally relax.

CHAPTER
TWENTY-SIX

AS THE PLAY ended the next evening, the audience gave the cast and crew a standing ovation.

Scared the Dickens Out of Me had gone off without a hitch.

Tali felt herself glowing inside. She wasn't happy for herself. But she was thrilled for Abby.

All the hard work her friend had put into the play had paid off. The audience had loved it.

As Tali looked out over the audience, she was pleased to see her niece, Maisie, had made it back in time. She also saw many people she recognized from around town.

Joe brought Abby some flowers from the cast and crew and then everyone came out to take their bows.

When they were done, Abby stepped forward to give a speech.

"I'm proud to say that we were able to raise more than six thousand dollars that we'd like to donate to Hope House," Abby said. "Everyone really stepped up tonight and more donations were made in the boxes at the back of the theater. Thank you all for your truly giving spirit."

Ty came forward to accept the money from her, offering a handshake and a hug.

Thankfully, the police had found the cash in Debbie's house and returned it to Abby.

"And I couldn't have done this without a lot of people, including Serena and Cadence," Abby continued. "You've really helped me through the difficult time I've had leading up to the play. But I especially could not have done this without my friends Tali and Mayor Mac. Could you two please come forward?"

Tali felt herself blush. She glanced at Mac, and he took her hand as they stepped out onto the front of the stage.

"These two have been my sanity the past couple of days, and this play wouldn't have happened without them," Abby continued. "If you could all just give them another round of applause, please."

Tali grinned as everyone around them stood once more and began to clap and cheer.

Mac squeezed her hand as he stood beside her.

Once the applause died, Mac turned to address the audience.

"Actually, I think this town is who we should thank," he began. "You guys really know how to come together when you're needed. I'd like to thank everybody for pitching in and lending a hand. You're all the heroes right now. The people in this room are what make Lantern Beach great, and I'm proud to be your mayor."

Another round of applause worked through the audience.

Mac's face turned serious. "And because of that, I can't think of any better time or place to do this than right here, right now."

What was he talking about? Tali wondered. What was he about to do?

The next instant, Mac lowered himself to one knee and reached into his pocket to pull something out.

Her head began to spin.

Was this . . . ?

No, it couldn't be . . .

When she saw the ring, she knew it was.

"Tali Robinson, from the moment I met you, you've made me a better person." Mac's voice sounded scratchy with emotion. "You've revitalized something inside me that I'd long since thought was dead. I can't imagine living another day without you at my side. Goldie, would you do me the honor of becoming my wife?"

Tali didn't even have to think about her response.

"Yes! Yes, I am the one who is honored, Mac MacArthur." She threw her arms around him in a long hug.

He chuckled and, as he rose to his feet, he pulled back just enough to slip the ring onto her finger.

It was the perfect fit.

Tali stared at Mac a moment, tears glimmering in her eyes.

Everyone from the cast and crew crowded around them to offer congratulations.

But she hardly noticed.

Instead, all she could think about was her future with Mac.

"You just made me very happy," Mac leaned closer and murmured.

Even though everyone was around them, they somehow felt alone.

"I understand the feeling." Tali admired the ring again. "When?"

"Whenever you're ready."

She glanced around and realized that all the people she cared about the most were in the room. "How about now?"

Mac's eyebrows shot up. "Now?"

"I love the people here. The setting. Yes, why not now?"

"But you don't even have a bouquet."

At his words, Cadence thrust something into her hands.

It was the flowers she'd made out of the pages of the discarded books. She'd arranged them into a bouquet.

And they were beautiful.

"What about a marriage license?" Mac asked.

"I can help you with that," the Clerk of the Court said from the audience.

Everyone chuckled.

"But Sugar isn't here . . ." Tali shrugged.

"Actually . . ." Maisie stepped into the aisle, an oversized bag on her shoulder.

Sugar's head popped out, and he let out a bark.

Another round of chuckles filled the space.

Maisie released Sugar, and the dog ran to the stage.

Tali scooped him into her arms and held him close. Then she turned to Mac. "What do you say?"

"I'm all in."

"Then it looks like we're going to have a wedding."

Thirty minutes later, everything was in place. Tali still wore her white angel costume. Someone had given her a belt that she put around her waist to cinch the gown a little bit more.

Preacher Jack Wilson stood on the stage as Tali and Mac said their vows before the people of the town.

After saying "I do," Mac placed a long kiss on her lips.

As they stepped back, Tali grinned up at him. "You did all of this for me, and I'm still not sure what to get you for Christmas. I've been trying my hardest to come up with the perfect gift idea."

"Not to start quoting songs again, but . . . all I want for Christmas is you."

Tali giggled.

And she knew that this Christmas was going to be a very happy Christmas indeed.

~~~

Thank you so much for reading *Bound by Mayhem.* If you enjoyed this book, please consider leaving a review!

COMPLETE BOOK LIST

Squeaky Clean Mysteries:

#14 Cold Case: Clean Sweep

#15 Cold Case: Clean Break

#16 Cleans to an End

While You Were Sweeping, A Riley Thomas Spinoff

The Sierra Files:

#1 Pounced

#2 Hunted

#3 Pranced

#4 Rattled

The Gabby St. Claire Diaries (a Tween Mystery series):

The Curtain Call Caper

The Disappearing Dog Dilemma

The Bungled Bike Burglaries

The Worst Detective Ever

#1 Ready to Fumble

#2 Reign of Error

#3 Safety in Blunders

#4 Join the Flub

#5 Blooper Freak

#6 Flaw Abiding Citizen

#7 Gaffe Out Loud

#8 Joke and Dagger

#9 Wreck the Halls

#10 Glitch and Famous

Raven Remington

Relentless

Holly Anna Paladin Mysteries:

#1 Random Acts of Murder

#2 Random Acts of Deceit

#2.5 Random Acts of Scrooge

#3 Random Acts of Malice

#4 Random Acts of Greed

#5 Random Acts of Fraud

#6 Random Acts of Outrage

#7 Random Acts of Iniquity

Lantern Beach Mysteries

#1 Hidden Currents

#2 Flood Watch

#3 Storm Surge

#4 Dangerous Waters

#5 Perilous Riptide

#6 Deadly Undertow

Lantern Beach Romantic Suspense

Tides of Deception

Shadow of Intrigue

Storm of Doubt

Winds of Danger

Rains of Remorse

Torrents of Fear

Lantern Beach P.D.

On the Lookout

Attempt to Locate

First Degree Murder

Dead on Arrival

Plan of Action

Lantern Beach Escape

Afterglow (a novelette)

Lantern Beach Blackout

Dark Water

Safe Harbor

Ripple Effect

Rising Tide

Lantern Beach Guardians

Hide and Seek

Shock and Awe

Safe and Sound

Lantern Beach Blackout: The New Recruits

Rocco

Axel

Beckett

Gabe

Lantern Beach Mayday

Run Aground

Dead Reckoning

Tipping Point

Lantern Beach Blackout: Danger Rising

Brandon

Dylan

Maddox

Titus

Lantern Beach Christmas

Silent Night

Crime á la Mode

Dead Man's Float

Milkshake Up

Bomb Pop Threat

Banana Split Personalities

Beach Bound Books and Beans Mysteries

Bound by Murder

Bound by Disaster
Bound by Mystery
Bound by Trouble
Bound by Mayhem

Vanishing Ranch

Forgotten Secrets
Necessary Risk
Risky Ambition
Deadly Intent
Lethal Betrayal
High Stakes Deception
Fatal Vendetta
Troubled Tidings

The Sidekick's Survival Guide

The Art of Eavesdropping
The Perks of Meddling
The Exercise of Interfering
The Practice of Prying
The Skill of Snooping
The Craft of Being Covert

Saltwater Cowboys

Saltwater Cowboy
Breakwater Protector
Cape Corral Keeper

Seagrass Secrets

Driftwood Danger

Unwavering Security

Beach House Mysteries

The Cottage on Ghost Lane

The Inn on Hanging Hill

The House on Dagger Point

School of Hard Rocks Mysteries

The Treble with Murder

Crime Strikes a Chord

Tone Death

Carolina Moon Series

Home Before Dark

Gone By Dark

Wait Until Dark

Light the Dark

Taken By Dark

Suburban Sleuth Mysteries:

Death of the Couch Potato's Wife

Fog Lake Suspense:

Edge of Peril

Margin of Error

Brink of Danger

Line of Duty

Legacy of Lies

Secrets of Shame

Refuge of Redemption

Cape Thomas Series:

Dubiosity

Disillusioned

Distorted

Standalone Romantic Mystery:

The Good Girl

Suspense:

Imperfect

The Wrecking

Sweet Christmas Novella:

Home to Chestnut Grove

Standalone Romantic-Suspense:

Keeping Guard

The Last Target

Race Against Time

Ricochet

Key Witness

Lifeline

High-Stakes Holiday Reunion

Desperate Measures

Hidden Agenda

Mountain Hideaway

Dark Harbor

Shadow of Suspicion

The Baby Assignment

The Cradle Conspiracy

Trained to Defend

Mountain Survival

Dangerous Mountain Rescue

Nonfiction:

Characters in the Kitchen

Changed: True Stories of Finding God through Christian Music (out of print)

The Novel in Me: The Beginner's Guide to Writing and Publishing a Novel (out of print)

ABOUT THE AUTHOR

USA Today has called Christy Barritt's books "scary, funny, passionate, and quirky."

Christy writes both mystery and romantic suspense novels that are clean with underlying messages of faith. Her books have sold more than three million copies and have won the Daphne du Maurier Award for Excellence in Suspense and Mystery, have been twice nominated for the Romantic Times Reviewers' Choice Award, and have finaled for both a Carol Award and Foreword Magazine's Book of the Year.

She is married to her Prince Charming, a man who thinks she's hilarious—but only when she's not trying to be. Christy is a self-proclaimed klutz, an avid music lover who's known for spontaneously bursting into song, and a road trip aficionado.

When she's not working or spending time with her family, she enjoys singing, playing the guitar, and exploring small, unsuspecting towns where people have no idea how accident-prone she is.

Find Christy online at:
www.christybarritt.com
www.facebook.com/christybarritt
www.twitter.com/cbarritt

Sign up for Christy's newsletter to get information on all of her latest releases here: **www.christybarritt. com/newsletter-sign-up/**

Made in United States
Orlando, FL
06 February 2024